OF PIXIES AND SPELLS

EMMA HAMM

CHAPTER 1

What does a hero do when there's no one left to save?

Freya found it was a lot of sitting around and talking. To anyone who would listen to her, although most of her visitors wanted to hear yet another part of her story.

The faeries already knew all the stories she'd told. They still wanted to hear them a thousand times over. If they could have played the stories on repeat, they would have. Mostly it was goblins who made their way to the Goblin King's castle. They slipped in through the cracks in the walls and then hunted her down for their daily fix.

But today, Freya didn't want to talk to any of the furry little creatures. She wanted a little time to herself.

If she was being honest with herself, time to herself was all she got these days.

Esther was very busy with Lux. While they were gone in the Winter Court, the two of them had stepped up in a big way to make sure the courts ran smoothly. They'd become a sort of go between for a lot of the faerie creatures. Esther was kind enough to understand their individual points of view from each court, and Lux could translate their words into something the other faeries understood.

Obviously, her sister and Lux didn't have time to visit Freya.

She could visit Arrow. He loved it when she came to his little home, even making her tea, though she hated every drop.

But he had gotten into the Goblin King's library and the faithful dog had disappeared. Now, whenever she tried to talk to him, all he wanted to speak of was the newest fact he'd discovered in between the pages of an old tome.

She found that information interesting most of the time. But there was only so much old history a woman could take.

And Eldridge? Well. Eldridge was busy being king. He didn't have time to entertain her, nor did it feel right to drag him away from it all.

Nearly every court needed his help to put their kingdoms back together after the Goblin Queen had destroyed many of them. The crumbling she'd seen in the Goblin Court had spread in their absence. Everyone had broken houses. Fractured court systems. Things that needed fixing and only the king could force them to work together.

She admired him for his patience. But she missed him a bit.

Freya left the castle in the stars and strode into the gardens. Eldridge kept many wild plants here that grew nowhere else. And it was one of the few peaceful places in the castle. She sat on a stone bench carved with twin lions and tilted her face back to the sun.

Her life here wasn't all that bad. She should have been happy to have a few relaxing months to herself. After all, it had been a very long time of fighting with the faeries.

She'd had to save her sister. Then had to get the king back after her actions had nearly destroyed all the courts in one fell swoop. She was a busy woman.

But it still felt like she was missing something. At home, at least, she had things to do. Freya was never still for very long in that cabin in the woods. The wards needed tending. The garden needed weeding. Most of the time she had to crawl on her hands and knees into the basement of the house just to get some wild creature away from their cold storage. She was busy all the time, and there was never a shortage of things to do.

Here, she touched nothing. All the items in the faerie courts were magical. Eldridge had made that very clear. If she wanted to blow herself up, then she could go about and poke whatever she wanted. But if she desired her fingers to remain attached to her hands, then she wouldn't touch unfamiliar objects.

So she'd stayed in her room. Like a good little human pet, waiting for when Eldridge would tell her she could leave. Except that moment never came.

She mused that she was now a princess locked away in a castle. Incapable of doing anything other than waiting for her prince to come and save her. Or, in her case, a king.

Freya opened a single eye at the sound of scuttling footsteps and stared down the small stone path that led back to the castle. A little goblin child stood in the middle with wide eyes, staring at her as if she might bite.

"Hello," she breathed. "What are you doing here?"

"Well." The boy was part cat, part human child. He had long whiskers on his face that bounced when he talked. Lifting a paw, he licked it and then rubbed behind his enormous ears. "My friend said that the woman who defeated the Goblin Queen lived here. He said you would be in the gardens but... You don't look like the lady who could do all that."

"I don't?" She lifted a brow. "And just what must this paragon look like?"

He lifted his paws into the air and flexed his claws. Sharp claws flashed in the sunlight. "She'd have claws like these."

"Oh." Freya nodded sagely. "Of course she would. And what else?"

"Um..." The little boy looked up, then back down. Finally, he used his paws to push back his lips and showed his long canines. "She'd have fangs like this!"

Or at least, that's what Freya thought he said. The garbled words were a little difficult to understand.

She supposed if someone was going to believe that the Goblin Queen was a monster, then it must take another monster to beat her. Freya wished she knew how to change her shape so that she could impress the child. But he wasn't the first to be a little disappointed when he met her.

Smiling, she shrugged. "I don't know what to tell you then. I'm the one who killed the Goblin Queen, and I don't have claws, fangs, horns, or other animal appendages, I'm afraid."

"You?" His eyes opened so wide they nearly fell out of his head. "You're the Queen Killer?"

Freya winced. She hated that nickname. The faeries had been trying it out for size, and she didn't know how to ask them to stop. It was a name that brought with it sad memories and guilt.

She didn't want to be known as the Queen Killer. Just Freya was fine. Or maybe the Goblin King's... friend?

No, that was a horrible path to go down. The last thing she needed was to be wondering what she was to the Goblin King when he had made it clear he didn't know the answer to that question either.

Sighing, she patted the bench beside her. "Why don't you come sit down? I'll tell you anything you want to hear."

"Really?"

"Really."

The goblin boy bounded to her side, plopped himself down on the bench with purpose, then hauled his tail out from under him to hold. "Did you want to kill the Queen?"

Freya blinked at the child. That was the first time anyone had asked her that question before. "Um..." She narrowed her eyes and furrowed her brow. "Why do you want to know that?"

"Well..." He looked side to side, then whispered, "I think killing a person must be hard, is all. And if you wanted to kill her, that would make you a lot scarier."

Oh, her heart was breaking for this soft hearted child. He

deserved to be showered with praise for the massive heart he hid in his cat-like chest. Leaning close, she whispered, "Do you promise not to tell anyone?"

His eyes widened even more, if that were possible. Nodding frantically, he stared into her eyes with slitted, dilated pupils.

Freya hoped she wouldn't disappoint him by telling the truth. "No. I didn't want to kill her. But sometimes there's no other option for bad people."

He nodded, although there was a question in his eyes he obviously didn't feel comfortable asking. "Did it feel weird?"

"Did what feel weird?"

"Killing someone." He looked down at his hands, then back up at her. "It's just... Well. My father died a while ago, and someone said that was because an elf had killed him. They said he deserved it, but..."

She didn't think her heart could hurt anymore, but there it went. Hurting even worse for this little boy who had lost a loved one. And his father, of all people? A boy needed his father.

How did she go about this without causing the child even more pain? Clearing her throat, she tried her best. "I think that would be a different situation, don't you? The Winter Princess was a horrible monster. She would have hurt all the faeries in every court if we didn't kill her. I don't think your father could have been that bad."

"He wasn't." The goblin boy tugged on the fabric of his pants. "I liked him."

"Then I don't think it's the same. Your father isn't like the Winter Princess." Freya wrapped her arm around his shoulders and leaned back against the bench with him. "How about we stay quiet for a little while? You can count all the birds that fly by."

"I do like birds!"

They waited in silence for all of ten heartbeats before the boy started rambling again. But at least this time he wasn't talking about how his father had been killed. He named every bird that flew by them. Some of them were nonsense, others were merely the species, but some he took the time to give proper names.

And when she was about ready to go mad from the imagination, this child held within him, the boy sighed. "I should go home. My mother probably misses me."

"Did you tell her you were going to sneak into the castle?" Freya knew the answer before he said it.

"No, of course not. She would have told me not to come, and then I never would have met the Queen Killer." He hopped off the bench and started down the path like he didn't need to even say goodbye. Like he was confident he would eventually see her again.

Leaning back on the bench, she let the sun play across her face. Though the boy's story had been sad, at least he could return to his mother. She'd likely be angry when he made his way back to their little home. But if she was anything like Freya's mother had been, then she would still hug the child tight with happiness that he'd made it home. Even if he'd lied about where he was going all day.

Her heart twisted in her chest at the thought of her mother.

Her mother, who was alive. Somewhere.

Freya couldn't find her though. She had to rely on other people to find information on the woman who had birthed her. The Autumn Thief understood the need for finding out information quickly. But it would never be quick enough.

Who knew what the Spring Maiden had done to her mother? Was that why she was so interested in Freya to begin with?

She ran her fingers through her hair in frustration. Whatever good feelings the goblin boy had brought disappeared in the wake of her mother's predicament. All Freya wanted to do was run out into the wilds and fight everyone who knew nothing about her mother's whereabouts.

But that wouldn't change her situation.

All she could do was sit. And wait. And hope that the faeries were doing whatever they could to find her mother. Even though she knew the likelihood of that was slim.

"Time for another walk, I guess," she snarled. Freya stood up. The anger shaking through her frame couldn't be contained, and the only way she knew how to ease the feeling was to walk.

So she did what she had been doing for too long. What she'd been doing every day since she returned to the Goblin King's court.

She walked.

CHAPTER 2

Freya realized she could no longer spend time indoors. She worried too much about what cursed object she would touch. So the Goblin King gave her freedom to travel throughout his kingdom, and it was easy to find places to sit and think.

Lately, she had taken to wandering all the way to the very edge of his kingdom where a small stream had split through his wards. The water wasn't magical. It wasn't sent by another person to attack the king, or even a risk to be near at all. The stream was shallow, simple, and the tiny eddies that swirled through it were lovely and relaxing.

Leaves from the Autumn Court danced on top of the water. They were little boats meandering their way down the stream to wherever it exited. She wasn't sure where it went. Freya had never followed it, but that was part of the appeal.

Not knowing where the water went gave her some semblance of normalcy. She wasn't the hero of this story anymore. She was just Freya. And as a normal woman in these parts, she probably shouldn't know what was going to happen or where everything went.

Sighing, she leaned back on her hands and watched the leaves twirl on their wild ride down the water. Someday, she would like to ride on a ship through the sea. Maybe she would even visit some strange faerie land like she had seen off the shores of the Summer Court.

The adventurous thoughts stalled when she remembered the major problem standing in her way.

Her mother.

The memory always darkened whatever dreams ran through Freya's head. Her beloved mother was missing and there was nothing she could do about it.

She had to sit here, with her hands tied, hoping someone would do what was right. And it was downright frustrating. If she didn't get some kind of information or relief from this torment, then she was certain she would go mad.

A leaf fell from above her head. Bright crimson and so vibrant she wondered if it were on fire. It floated through the air like a snowflake. Not that she'd ever be able to look at snowflakes the same again. Not after her time in the Winter Court.

A hand appeared out of nowhere, snatching the leaf midair and holding the lovely foliage in front of her eyes. "Were you staring at this so intently because you wanted it? I could make it last forever if it's leaves that you want."

Eldridge stepped in front of her. He wore his customary black suit with golden embroidery on the shoulders. The sun turned his black hair into an oil slick color of blues, purples, and hidden reds.

He'd gained weight since they returned to the Goblin Court. Finally. After months of torture at the hands of the Goblin Queen, it had taken a while for him to return to his normal handsome nature.

Now, it was hard to even look at him. He was too attractive. Too otherworldly. Suddenly a Goblin King once again, and not just someone she had to save.

Taking a deep breath, Freya reached for the leaf and held it by the stem. Twirling it in her hand, she tried to appreciate the gift for what it was. An olive branch. Eldridge and her hadn't been themselves lately.

She supposed it was to be expected after what they'd gone through.

"It's lovely," she replied. "And surprising to see anything from Autumn in your court."

"Did you think it would be all darkness and gloom?" He flipped the tails of his coat up and sat down on the ground beside her.

She hadn't expected him to risk getting the suit dirty and noticed how he hid a wince. Eldridge had important news, that much was apparent. Otherwise, he never would have sat on the dirty ground.

Or something else had gone wrong, and he needed to be on the same level with her so she didn't tackle him to the ground.

Immediately suspicious, Freya turned toward him and asked, "What happened?"

His eyes widened in surprise. "Nothing happened! Why would you even suggest that? Nothing at all has happened. I just wanted to visit with you. It's been a while since we had time to ourselves and... well." He struggled to find his next words, only to throw up his hands and shrug.

That wasn't good either.

The Goblin King was never at a loss for words. And though she didn't want anything to be wrong, she was ashamed to admit her heart picked up its pace. If something was wrong, that meant they needed her. That she was still someone to go to when the faeries needed help.

Even though she'd never been that person in the first place.

She sighed and tried to think of something to say to him. Something that would pull out the words he wanted to tell her, even though he didn't know how to say them.

Freya settled on gesturing all around them. "The sun is shining, Goblin King. The stream is burbling and the leaves are falling like rain around us. This is a beautiful setting to say something difficult, so you might as well spit it out. I don't think you'll get a better chance than this."

Though he obviously was still struggling, Eldridge relented. "You don't seem like yourself, Freya. That's all. You wander around my kingdom with a lost expression on your face, and I don't know how to help you. I want to, you know."

"But you're busy being king." She broke away from the hope in his gaze and stared down at her fingers she'd twisted in her lap. "You have more important things to focus on than a human woman you picked up on your travels."

At her words, Eldridge lunged forward. He shifted until he was on his knees before her, then reached out for her hands. He squeezed them tight between his own. "Freya, that is not how I feel about you. Surely you know that you are so much more than some stray I picked up in my wanderings around the kingdom."

Did she?

Logically, yes. They had a connection between them now. Their travels would have attached most people, though. She felt a connection with Arrow as well and wondered if the romantic feelings were only lacking because he was a dog.

Her thoughts were all messed up in her head. Jumbled like she had thrown them all into a bucket and shook them around too hard.

But leaving him on his knees, though highly appealing, felt wrong too. Eldridge needed to know what was going on in her head, especially if she was distracting him from being king.

"I know," she replied, shaking her head and squeezing his fingers in return. "I just can't focus on anything when I know my mother is out there. She's waiting for me to find her, or maybe she's stuck in that horrible nightmare realm. There's a thousand possibilities of what is going on. How am I supposed to do anything? Think of anything but her suffering?"

He released his hold on her hands and moved a lock of hair behind her ear. His fingers lingered, warm and smooth and comforting. "You are a hero at heart, Freya of Woolwich. I should have known your wandering soul wouldn't want to linger here for long."

She supposed that was a way to look at it, although it didn't feel right either. Freya wasn't just some wandering soul. She was a daughter who feared for her mother. Simple as that.

But could a faerie ever understand that suffering? She'd never seen them show any familial ties at all. Even when it came to killing their adoptive sister.

That dark memory haunted her, too.

It seemed like she couldn't get away from her sins. All the memories of what she'd done, where she'd been, how she'd beaten two very powerful faeries. They all lingered until she didn't know which way was up and which way was down.

And the guilt, as well. A wonderful, talented, strange man knelt before her, begging for her attention and for Freya to return to normal. This was her chance to see what a life with the Goblin King would really be like.

She'd ruin all this if she didn't dig herself out of this hole.

Freya opened her mouth to apologize, but no words came out. She just stared at him with her eyes wide, hoping that he would understand what she was trying to convey.

She needed time.

To find her mother.

To feel like the hero in her own life again. Faeries be damned. She needed something to happen that would return her power.

He slid his hand from behind her head, down her neck, and stopped over the pounding beat of her heart. "I came here to tell you that I will never let you linger in the dark for long. Not alone. You must know that."

"I do." After all they'd been through, Freya trusted that he had her best interest at heart. He really wanted her to be happy here.

Namely because he assumed she still wanted to run back to the human realm. She didn't know how many times he'd asked her if she missed her little cabin. Freya even had to clarify with him if he was asking so much because he wanted her to leave.

He didn't. She had to remember that.

"Good," he replied with a soft smile on his face. "Then I want you to take what I have to say next as hope. Do you understand me?"

She shifted forward with excitement brewing in her chest. So he did have something to tell her. Something very important if he was certain she would take it wrong. "What is it?"

"We received a letter from someone I'm sure you will remember." He leaned away from her to pull a small piece of paper out of his pocket. "Apparently an old friend of ours knows where your mother is."

Heart racing in her chest, she reached for the letter he held in his grasp. An old friend? She didn't have many friends here, and she knew Arrow wouldn't have written a letter to them. The goblin dog would have stomped to the castle, radiating with anger.

"From who?" she asked, opening the envelope and pulling out a small card.

The smell hit her first. Like someone had thrown a bouquet of roses into her face. Then she saw the glitter on the edges of the card and she knew who had sent them the note.

Freya frowned and looked back at Eldridge. "The Spring Maiden?"

He nodded. Small, worried wrinkles appeared between his eyes. "Just read it, Freya."

The note had crumpled edges, likely from Eldridge's fists when he first read what the Spring Maiden had to say. Neither of them had fond memories of the leader of the Spring Court.

My dear Eldridge,

I know much time has passed since we last saw each other. I hope you've been well.

It's my understanding that you have in your charge a very unique mortal woman. I have also met this fine creature and only realized recently that I know where a certain motherly figure to this woman resides.

Just thought you'd like to know.

If you find yourself curious, come and visit for a while, would you? It's been too long since the Spring Court has seen the Goblin King.

Yours,

Spring Maiden.

Freya frowned at the signature. "Why would the Spring Maiden reach out after all this time? She never mentioned my mother while I was there. Did she mention her to you?"

Eldridge shook his head and stood up. He held out his hand for her to take while replying, "No. Even when I was hiding myself as one of her guards, I never heard her say a single thing about another mortal woman."

A letter like this made little sense, then. Freya took his hand belatedly and let him pull her up to his side. She stared at the letter, trying to piece together this mystery even though she didn't have enough information to do so.

"I just don't understand," she muttered. "Why now?"

With a muttered curse, Eldridge plucked the paper from her grip.

Freya let out a snarl of frustration and reached for it again. They held it between them, tugging back and forth until she finally let go before it tore. "Eldridge, what are you doing? I need to figure out why she sent the letter."

"And we will." He wrapped an arm around her waist and tugged her against his chest. "This is more fire in you than I've seen since we beat the Winter Princess. Let me enjoy the battle between us for a moment."

All the wind blew out of her sails. Yes, she supposed she had been rather boring while she was trying to forget all the bad things that had happened.

Freya placed her hands on his shoulders. She smoothed her fingers over the muscles beneath his jacket, feeling them shift and twitch at her touch. "I've been rather boring, haven't I?"

"You don't know how to sit still." He lowered his head, lips so close to hers she could feel their heat. "But I missed this side of you, my hero."

"Don't call me that when no one needs saving." Freya leaned closer, flirting with touching him but never quite letting their lips finally do what they both wanted.

And she did still want to kiss him. Every fiber of her being wanted to lean in, press their lips together, and let him warm her from the outside in.

Maybe she could. Just this once. Even though she still didn't feel like herself, maybe kissing him would make her feel a little more like the hero he kept calling her. She could be that person again, if only she gave herself the chance.

She leaned forward, eyes drifting shut.

Eldridge slid a hand between them and pressed a finger to her lips, stopping them from ever touching his.

Freya's eyes popped open again, flying wide in shock.

Mischief danced in his gaze. "There will be time for that, my dear."

"There's time for it now."

"Perhaps, but isn't the wait that much more delicious?" He released her with that wicked smile on his face. "We have to go see the Spring Maiden, you know. There's a lot of planning to do. And packing! My goodness, we have to pack half the castle if I'm to come with you."

"Why would you come with me?" She shook her head to clear the fog of desire from her mind. "We're trying to find my mother, not yours."

"I would certainly hope she isn't my mother. That would make all this attraction between us very awkward." He danced out of her reach, nearly falling into the stream behind him in his excitement. "Come on, Freya! Back to the castle we go. Adventure waits for no hero."

She followed him with a smile on her face for the first time in what felt like forever. He was a ridiculous man. A foolish man, even.

But she hoped someday she could call him hers.

CHAPTER 3

She stood in the courtyard of the Goblin King's castle, a place she hadn't realized existed, and blew at the hair that fell in front of her face. "We're traveling in that?"

A carriage stood before her. A normal, entirely mortal carriage. Or at least, similar enough that she knew what it was without having to clarify. The wooden sides were black, not painted, but actual black wood. But the wheels were normal. The horses were normal as well. They stamped their hooves in impatience at the goblin man at the front of the carriage. He held onto the reins and stared straight ahead, rabbit ears twitching at her question.

Eldridge stopped beside her and adjusted the sleeves of his midnight blue suit. "Yes, of course. Did you think we were going to walk to the Spring Court? That would take all day."

All day?

She twitched the pale blue skirt of her traveling gown. "I've always traveled through portals to get from one court to the next."

"Yes, I remember. Arrow loves his portals because he's deathly afraid of horses. And the two of you were in a rather large hurry to get between each of them, were you not?" He nodded at the horses again. "I don't mind a few hours of travel, and I assumed bringing all our belongings would be a little easier this way than having to travel through the portal eight times. I brought a lot of clothing, Freya."

She knew he had packed more outfits than she could count, but... "How close is the Spring Court to yours?"

With a sigh of impatience, Eldridge shaded his eyes with his hand and stared off to their right. "About a few hours by carriage ride that way. You can't see it from here because the trees block that dreadful garden the Spring Maiden loves so much."

"I..." She blinked, then swallowed hard. "I didn't realize all the courts were so close to each other."

"They're close to my kingdom, if that's what you mean. The Goblin King has to be between all of them, so they all touch the land that is officially mine, even though no one lives here other than me." Eldridge winked. "I'm glad there are still things in my kingdom that can surprise you, Freya."

"It's never boring in the faerie realms," she agreed. She took his offered arm and let him lead her down the steps to the side of the carriage, although she was still a little surprised.

All the courts touched this land? They were really all that close to each other?

The goblin at the front nodded to her. The bubbles of his cheeks moved up and down, like a rabbit sniffing at something. She could only assume that was a smile as Eldridge opened the door and tucked her inside.

This was really a lovely carriage. The interior had been painted with a thousand stars and a bright galaxy above her head. The dark cushions were comfortable and the plush back cupped her spine. Magic. She would never get over how useful it was to have in her everyday life.

The carriage shifted as Eldridge entered. He settled himself and then tapped the ceiling.

Off they went. Too easily and far too simplistic for her liking.

Freya stared out the small window, then looked back at the Goblin King. "We're the only ones going?"

"Yes."

She chewed her lip. "Won't we need some of the others to help us? The Spring Maiden is very untrustworthy. We both know that."

Was he trying to hide a smile?

He took a few moments to reply to her, staring out the window with his hand pressed against his mouth. Finally he said, "This is a political meeting. She's a court leader who has officially invited her king to come see her. I don't think we need to show up with an army at her doorstep."

"What if this is a trick, though?" Freya didn't trust any faerie leader other than him. And mostly she didn't trust the Goblin King either. "She could be trying to take the throne, just like the Winter Princess."

"Dahlia is not so powerful that she could ever take the throne. If she managed to kill me, it would go to the Summer Lord now that the Winter Princess is dead." He leaned back in his seat.

"That doesn't mean she wouldn't try to kill both of you then. I think we should at least bring Arrow, or let him know where we're going." Her heart raced. Was this another situation when he underestimated his opponent? What if the Spring Maiden had cooked up this plan to take out all the court leaders in one fell swoop?

Was it hot in the carriage? She was hot.

Eldridge nudged her foot with his own. "Freya. Not everyone is out to kill me. I know the Winter Princess might have made you think that, but there has been no struggle between the courts since I became King. You don't have to worry so much."

But she did. Because he wasn't worrying at all, and someone had to think of these things or... or...

He tapped her toes hard. Nearly stomping on her foot to make his point. "Freya, I realize I've given you no reason to think faeries aren't warring creatures lacking hearts. I know your experience with us thus far has been trickery and strife. But we are very similar to the nobles in your realm. Not everything is about battle and winning wars."

How did she tell him that she didn't trust his judgement? After their experience in the Winter Court, and her own experience with him, it didn't seem likely that her opinion of them was wrong. Sure, his experiences differed from hers.

Eldridge forgot Freya was mortal. The Spring Maiden didn't like her kind. She was more likely to have Freya's mother locked away in a dreaming world to watch her memories than actually know where her mother was.

This was a trick. She was certain of it.

If the Goblin King didn't want to believe that, then she would just have to be that more on her guard. Ready for anything, no matter what that cost her.

"Freya," he repeated. "The worst we can expect is that she'll want something in return for information about your mother. This is the same kind of deal the Autumn Thief has been helping us make across the kingdom. We haven't come up with anything real. If anyone would know about a mortal in their court, it would be the person who leads it. Don't you think?"

Her thoughts must have played across her features like an open book. Eldridge rolled his eyes with a grin and stared out the window for the remainder of their ride. And that was fine. Freya didn't want to talk when she had to plan how to keep them both alive.

The landscape was a little distracting, though. Even she had to admit it.

Autumn was the theme of the Goblin Kingdom, although it was a little darker than the Autumn Court itself. She watched the sky move from twilight into the bright morning of the Spring Court. The moment they entered the Spring Maiden's kingdom was painfully obvious.

The ground shifted into emerald green like someone had

unrolled an impressive carpet. Flowers dotted through the grass, bright and almost too vivid to be real. Fluffy white clouds danced through the sky. Birds started singing. Their chirping warbles reminded her of her time in this place, and how easy it had been for the Spring Maiden to capture her mind.

Freya shivered.

"Remembering your last visit?" Eldridge asked.

"Yes." She pointed to some of the pavilions just out of sight. "I remember those a little too well. They had me laid out like I was nothing more than convenient entertainment."

Eldridge frowned, his own memories turning his expression dark. "I've always hated the way the Spring Maiden sees your kind. She thinks mortals are weak minded, but idolizes your lives. The two don't fit, but she would never explain her thinking to me."

"I don't think she wants to be one of us. I think she's just fascinated with the way other people live." At least the Spring Maiden had been kinder than the Winter Princess. The Spring Court was more about satisfying their strange leader's needs. And less about causing other people pain.

"Don't give her so much credit." He touched a finger to the side of his face where thorns had broken through his skin. "There's a lot I need to talk with her about, and one of those things will be her treatment of the guards."

The words were refreshing. At least someone was going to hold the court leaders accountable for the pain they had caused.

Leaning forward, she placed her hand on his knee and squeezed. "I had completely forgotten you immersed yourself in this court to watch over me. More than anyone, you would know of the pain here."

"Every court likes to cause pain. Such desires are part of who we are as faeries." His eyes darkened. He stared at her like he wanted to take a bite out of her, but Freya didn't think he would.

He'd always been so gentle with her. So calm when he could

have been forceful and rough. Surely he wasn't one of the faeries who liked pain...

Was he?

Considering the light in his eyes, she feared she might be wrong. Perhaps that was the reason he'd put some space between them.

Leaning back in her seat, she shoved her spine hard against the back of the carriage. If he wanted pain, then she didn't know if she could go through with this. Freya knew nothing about the acts of love. Let alone causing another person pain.

It was a lot to think about. Maybe too much, when she rolled it over in her mind.

Eldridge wrapped his knuckles against the ceiling, hard. She jumped at the sound, thinking he was mad at her or warning her of what was to come. But he was just letting the goblin man know that they were stopping.

Suddenly, she found herself a little fearful of the Goblin King all over again. And that wasn't fair to him. Not after everything they'd gone through.

Freya would look deeper into that reaction later. But for now, she needed to be on guard in the Spring Court. "Stopping so soon?"

"The Spring Maiden doesn't let anyone enter her court much farther than this. Even the Goblin King." He threw the door to the carriage open and stepped out. "Come along, Freya. Someone will find us soon enough, and then the game is on."

She could only imagine that game would be difficult to play.

She exited the carriage and waved goodbye to the goblin man as he steered it back the way they had come. He gave her another odd smile that was more a bouncing of cheeks than anything else.

At least the goblins liked her now. Freya considered that to be a success.

The Goblin King straightened his coat one last time. She had seen him do the action so many times, but now she wondered if it was a nervous tick. He always seemed to check and make sure he was presentable before he took on another adventure.

If he was nervous, then at least she knew he wouldn't do anything foolish.

Freya stepped up to his side and put her hand on his arm. "You said someone would find us?"

He jumped at her touch. "Ah. Yes. The Spring Maiden has wards at her borders that tell her servants when someone arrives. They're the ones who greeted you the last time, if you remember."

"I do." She squeezed his bicep. "I didn't know you were watching even then."

The anxiety in his gaze eased. He reached up and placed his hand over hers. "I was watching you the entire time, Freya. Even in the moments when you felt like you were alone."

God, if that didn't heat her to the very core. She wanted to kiss him badly. She wanted to jump into his arms and say they didn't need to find the Spring Maiden yet. If only they could have a few moments when she could prove to him that even though she had been distracted, she still wanted him.

Someone cleared their throat, interrupting her thoughts. "Goblin King. It's been a very long time since you entered the court."

They both turned to see a pixie behind them. The strange creature pulsed its wings slowly, the dragonfly texture casting rainbow beams onto the surrounding flowers.

She'd forgotten how beautiful the spring faeries were. This one had golden curls tangling down to her bottom, with a heart-shaped pale face that reflected the sun. She wore a lovely, short dress made of spiderwebs.

They were so fragile in appearance. Freya always wanted to ask if they needed help walking, but she supposed that was part of their dangerous magic. Pixies didn't need help. Their mouths were full of razor-sharp teeth and they moved with unnatural speed.

If anyone needed help in the Spring Court, it would be Freya.

Eldridge squeezed her hand one last time. "It has been a long time. However, the Spring Maiden summoned us. We're here for a visit."

The pixie looked Freya up and down, then bared her sharp teeth in a smile. "I remember you. Your memories were so sweet to watch."

Freya gulped. "Thank you?"

Apparently there was nothing else the pixie had to say to the mortal. She turned around and waved a hand for them to follow her. "The Spring Maiden has been expecting you. I'm to show you all the changes in the kingdom, Goblin King. Then she will meet us at the end of your... tour."

They followed the pixie, and Eldridge leaned down to whisper in her ear, "Stalling? Maybe you were right, Freya. Something strange is happening here."

An icy shiver trailed down her spine. What could be happening in the Spring Court?

CHAPTER 4

The pixie led them through waist high flower fields.
Freya's nose filled with the scent of lavender and rose.
Once, she would have marveled at how lovely it all
smelled. But now she remembered the Spring Maiden's cursed
perfume and how it had made her do whatever the Spring
Maiden wanted.

She hated the thought that someone had controlled her so
easily. The spell had been intense and impossible to break.

If Eldridge hadn't saved her, she still would have been in
these fields entertaining the faeries with her memories.

She didn't want to think about what would have happened
then. These faeries hadn't necessarily been cruel to her. They
just hadn't seen her as anything other than a new toy to play
with. They thought mortals weren't alive, and that was part of
the problem.

She couldn't help herself. The pixie who guided them
through the gardens had claimed to remember her, but Freya
couldn't conjure up the face in her memories.

There was no other option. She had to ask. "I'm sorry, I don't
remember you. How do we know each other?"

The pixie grinned again, sharp teeth glinting in the sun. "My brother used to brush your hair. And when he was finished, and you fell back to sleep, I would braid it into a thousand tiny braids all over your head. You looked so lovely sleeping like that, you know. Much better than now."

Freya touched a hand to her loose hair. Sure, it was pin straight and falling around her shoulders. Maybe a few strands were frizzy, but she hadn't had time to think about her hair lately. She bathed. It was clean, and that was enough.

"My hair?" she asked. "I don't remember you braiding my hair."

"Like I said, mortal, you were asleep. So few of our flowers remember anything once they enter the dreaming realm." The pixie held out her arm for them to go ahead of her. "These are the new dreaming chambers. After you left, the Spring Maiden realized there were a few flaws in the original design. We've completely remade them."

Freya didn't want to know what they had created. These pavilions were always so dangerous to begin with, but she didn't remember any flaws. She hadn't escaped from them at all, so surely they had functioned appropriately?

Apparently she was wrong.

What had once been an open area was now closed off. The dreaming person was held down onto the bed by a hundred vines that shifted and moved while they slept. The thick tendrils looked like garden snakes writhing over the prone form of the poor man who had laid down to sleep.

A leaf touched his cheek tenderly, then moved again as it continued in the strange, wrapping coil.

At least the man was asleep. Freya thought if he had awoken and seen what was happening to him, he might have screamed in fear.

"Why did you change it?" Curiosity got the better of her. And she felt more brave with the Goblin King standing beside her. "At least before I could wake up a few times and breathe fresh air."

"The Spring Maiden realized that was the flaw. You were only able to escape because she let you wake up and play with us." The pixie touched a finger underneath her eye, wiping away an imaginary tear. "Now we don't get to play with them anymore. But at least we can still watch their dreams."

Freya shared a horrified glance with Eldridge.

He looked deeply disturbed by what they had found. And something in his gaze said he would speak with the Spring Maiden about this terrifying development as well.

Small consolation, but at least someone wanted to help these poor people.

Clearing her throat, Freya tried to get as much information as she could out of the pixie. "How many dreamers do you have? I remember there were quite a few of us."

The pixie grinned and shook her head. "You don't remember any such thing, Freya. You were sleeping. And when you weren't, the Spring Maiden's perfume kept you in a silly little stupor. Don't think it will be that easy to trick any of us. We're the ones who are masters at trickery, not you, mortal."

"Easy," the Goblin King snarled. "She is the hero of these courts. The one who saved us all from the icy grasp of the Winter Princess. You will offer her respect and nothing else, pixie, or I will rip your wings from your back."

Another person interrupted Eldridge, and the sound of her voice sent shivers down Freya's spine.

"Please don't threaten my pixies, Eldridge. Of all people, you should know how protective I am of my dear, darling creatures." The Spring Maiden rounded the corner of the pavilion. "You're just as protective as I am, my king."

Why did Freya feel like she had to curtsey? This woman had done nothing but haunt Freya's dreams for countless nights, and still she felt like she needed to offer respect.

The Spring Maiden was just as lovely as she remembered. The ethereal quality of her nature was the same, although perhaps her pale features were a little more drawn. Her white hair fell lank around her face, rather than shining with oil. And her clothing had more moth-eaten holes than Freya remembered.

In short, the Spring Maiden looked rather ragged. That in itself was a warning.

But just because the Spring Maiden was tired, didn't mean her teeth were gone. She moved in that blurry way that always made Freya ill. One moment, she was standing beside the sleeping man, and in the next, she was directly in front of Freya.

"Hello, my dear," the Spring Maiden rasped. "I don't think you know just how much I missed you and your lovely memories. They were a joy in the darkest of times."

Freya tried her very best to not flinch as the Spring Maiden dragged her claws down Freya's face. This was too close to what it had been like in her trap. And Freya hadn't realized how traumatic the experience had been until she returned.

Now, she remembered the feeling of drowning. How she had been stuck here with no one to save her, no hope at all. So of course she had fallen under the perfumed smell. She wanted to escape from this nightmare so badly that she would have done or taken anything that offered her some kind of relief.

Eldridge's hand snapped out from her left. He grabbed onto the Spring Maiden's wrist and forced her away from Freya's face. "I'm glad her memories were so satisfying then, Dahlia. But as I reminded your pixie, this is no longer a mortal woman who stumbled into your court. She saved us all, and you would do well to remember that."

Though his grip must have been punishing, the Spring Maiden merely smiled. Her teeth were sharper than their guide's. It was like looking into the mouth of a shark. "Yes, I understand what she did to Lumi. But I wanted to ask just how much input you had in those decisions? Weren't you and the Winter Princess close? How strange to hear she died just after capturing you."

He stiffened. "You know I had no hand in what happened."

"I think you did. After all this time ruling with you, Goblin

King, I know the signs of your hand. You killed another court leader, and that alone is enough to suspect your intentions in being here." Those teeth gnashed with every word. The Spring Maiden was only barely holding herself back from biting Eldridge. "Wouldn't that be a concern for all of us if you were trying to pick off the court leaders, one by one?"

"You know I'm not doing that," he snarled.

"I think you have a lot of plans, Goblin King. And I don't think any of those plans include us. So I wouldn't know what is going on in that head of yours." She stilled, the blurry motions that always radiated around her disappearing. "Perhaps if I could take a peek into that head of yours, I could tell the other leaders that you aren't plotting against us. I'm a more powerful ally than I am an enemy, Eldridge."

Oh no. If Eldridge got on one of those beds, then Freya knew damned well he would never wake up. She had just gotten him back. She refused to risk losing him again so soon.

She whipped out her own hand, grabbing onto the Spring Maiden's other wrist. She squeezed hard until the Spring Maiden's wrist turned bright red. "He's not letting you watch him dream. And you aren't going to peek into his head. He is the king of all the courts. Your king. You will give him the respect he deserves."

Perhaps the Spring Maiden hadn't thought a mortal could be so strong. Or perhaps Freya had come across even more aggressive than she'd planned. But whatever she'd done, she had surprised the Spring Maiden.

Those big blue eyes, with no whites at all, stared at her in shock. Blinked. And then the fine lines of movement rippled around the Spring Maiden once again. "You defend him with such passion when you hated him only a few months ago. What changed?"

"That's not for you to know," Freya snarled. "You're the one who called us here. Not for the courts. Not for Eldridge to undergo a firing squad of your own questions. You claimed to know something of my mother, and I will hear what you have to say. Anything else, I'm afraid you'll have to send another request for Eldridge to visit your court at a separate time."

"A mortal speaks for the king?" The Spring Maiden tilted her head back and laughed. One might think the two of them didn't have complete control over the Spring Maiden.

Eldridge shifted his grip, forcing the Spring Maiden's attention back to him. "Yes, she speaks for me. When one finds the other half of their soul, one keeps it."

He shouldn't have said that. Freya didn't even know where their relationship was going, or what would happen between the two of them. Why would he declare his feelings to a court leader? That should have stayed between the two of them until they could have talked about it a little more privately.

She was going to kill him. It was the only way to get out of this embarrassing situation and not feel her cheeks burn any longer.

The pixie behind them coughed into her hand. They had an audience of more than just their guide now. Pixies from all over the Spring Court had surrounded them without Freya noticing the veritable army the Spring Maiden had summoned.

And they had all heard what the Goblin King had said.

Freya was going to drag him into the first dark corner she could find. And she wasn't sure if she was going to hit him, kiss him, or do both in that order because he'd just declared them a couple. Without asking her permission. But her heart still fluttered in that odd little thump.

The Spring Maiden wriggled in their grip. "Well, if that's the way of it, let me go. No more games, Goblin King. I understand that you intend to find this woman's mother and stake your claim. Unhand me."

Oh no. He would not stake his claim when they found her mother. Freya didn't want anyone staking any claim over her. She was her own person.

Eldridge interjected before she could say anything that might insult the other woman. "We just want to find her mother first, Dahlia. Then we'll see about whatever I might have to say to the woman. You claimed to know where she is."

He released his hold on the Spring Maiden, so Freya reluctantly followed suit. She still wanted to squeeze the woman's arm for a little while longer, or at least until she could make the Spring Maiden feel the same way she had.

The pixie leader took a step back and shook out her hands. "Like the rest of the people you've asked, I've only heard rumors. But I won't tell you anything without a deal, you know that."

Eldridge nodded. "I understand. What do you want in return for information?"

The Spring Maiden licked her lips. She looked left and right, then gestured for the other pixies to leave. Not another word was said until they were alone, giving Freya enough time to realize two things.

First, the Spring Maiden looked worse for wear because she was exhausted. The deep bags under her eyes cast horrible shadows in the sunlight. And second, the Spring Maiden was afraid.

Very, very afraid.

When they were alone, the Spring Maiden leaned forward and rasped, "I need your help. I have to show you something, Goblin King. I don't think you will like it."

CHAPTER 5

The Spring Maiden led them away from the field of dreamers and down a smaller path lit by will-o'-the-wisps. Freya remembered these bridges with their tangled white roses covering them. It was just as beautiful as she remembered, although she couldn't decide if that was a good thing or not.

She felt like she should hate this place. Every inch of it was created to lure mortals into a lifetime of doom, and yet, she couldn't feel anything but awe.

The pixies here were terrifying, sure, but they were still faeries. Still part of the same whole that had created her dearest friend and now, the man that apparently everyone knew she was infatuated with.

"I can't believe you said that with everyone standing there," she hissed. "Now they all think we're... We're..."

"A couple?" He wrapped an arm around her shoulder and jostled her. "I know we haven't talked about it, but frankly I can't have you falling head over heels for yet another poor sap with a thorn mask."

"That's why you said it?" She was going to slap him. Where was that dark corner when she needed it? "Eldridge, I don't go around falling head over heels in general. Let alone for another guard."

"You tried to save me last time without even knowing who I was. I'm just making sure everyone knows you aren't available." He grinned, and the expression was far too satisfying on his face. "Besides, I like it when you argue with me. Your cheeks get all flushed and it's such a pretty color."

A childish part of her wanted to clap her hands to said cheeks so he wouldn't get any satisfaction from his argument. If he liked her pretty red cheeks, then he should only see them when he'd earned the right to do so.

For now, she was intent on making sure his ears blistered by the time she finished yelling at him.

"Lovebirds, this is highly entertaining and I would cherish listening further, but I need you to focus on me." The Spring Maiden had stopped at the end of the bridge and was waiting for them. "People tend to get lost in this part of my court, and Eldridge, I'm not all that confident you remember how to get to the castle."

"I remember," he grumbled, forcing his attention away from Freya and back to the woman waiting for them. "I'm not that dense."

"Well, we will have to agree to disagree. I remember you getting lost the last time you tried to find it, and I had to send all the pixies out to find you." She shook her head. "You'd think someone as powerful as the Goblin King would remember a few simple directions."

Eldridge released his hold on Freya and stomped toward the other faerie. "They weren't simple directions, Dahlia. You purposefully made them confusing so you could laugh at me."

"So you admit you couldn't find the castle on your own then?"

"I'm admitting nothing! I'm simply stating the facts. Unlike you, who seems very intent on making sure that I'm embarrassed in front of this woman." He pointed to Freya. "She knows me well enough to see right through your exaggerations. Freya, tell her."

She wasn't all that sure the Spring Maiden was wrong.

Looking between the two of them, Freya chose the safest option. "I think I'd very much like to see the castle of the Spring Court, and that standing here arguing is only delaying the inevitable. It doesn't matter which one of you is right."

His nostrils flared.

The Spring Maiden grinned and rolled her eyes. "I always liked you, Freya. Your memories were refreshing and I'm glad to see reality is the same. Come on, you two."

She raised her arms and whispered a few words. The hedges in front of them parted in a wave of movement, undulating under the Spring Maiden's power. The greenery revealed a land beyond that was unlike anything Freya would have guessed in this kingdom of spring.

A giant castle stood with twin stairways that arced away from the white marble structure. More gardens grew about this part of the Spring Court, but these weren't manicured like the others. All the plants here grew wild and free, without a single hand to cut them or change their natural shape.

Somehow, this made the land even more beautiful.

The castle itself was more like the ones she'd seen in the mortal realms. The shape was boxier, without the long parapets and twisting spires like the Goblin King's castle. This one was sturdy, meant to last through anything that befell it. And while that was unexpected for the beautiful Spring Maiden's court, it somehow fit the impressively strong woman she knew the Spring Maiden to be.

A few of her guards wandered past them, their faces covered by those strange masks. Eldridge's expression tightened.

If Freya didn't speak up, they were going to argue again and who knew how long it would last this time.

"Spring Maiden," she asked, her voice slightly panicked. "You said you knew where my mother was."

Of course, Freya had already figured out that wasn't what the Spring Maiden had meant in her letter. She'd already admitted she had no idea where her mother was, but that she had the means to find a lost mortal in her court.

The Spring Maiden glanced behind her, then replied, "I don't know exactly where she is. But I do know she's in my court. Surprisingly, we lost track of her for a while."

"How did she end up in the Spring Court?" Freya tried to piece together the story, but it just made little sense.

The portal behind her childhood home hadn't led to the Spring Court. It had placed Freya in an in-between place, waiting for another faerie to bring her somewhere else. That was how she had left it, at least. Arrow had helped guide her through the magic and to the Spring Court itself.

But her mother wouldn't have had such a guide. She wouldn't have had any way to get to the Spring Court, not without help, at least.

The Spring Maiden gestured to one of her guards, and he sprinted ahead of them toward the doors of the castle. Once he had opened them, the Spring Maiden replied, "She was looking for something. I don't know what, the pixie who brought her here didn't know what she wanted. But your mother did say that she was certain she could only find it in the Spring Court."

That, at least, made sense. Her mother was a collector of strange objects. It made sense that her curiosity and passion for magical items might bring her here. "Why do you think she's still here, then?"

The Spring Maiden turned around. Her strange eyes seemed to widen, but it wasn't with happiness or glee as Freya expected. No. The Spring Maiden's eyes were welling with tears. "My dear, I know when anyone enters or exits this court. There is not a single place in the entire Spring Kingdom that isn't warded. My borders are air tight and no one has ever broken them. I knew when your mother entered Spring, and I have no question that she never left this place."

The eerie words filled her with a sense of dread. If her mother had never left, then what was she supposed to do? How was she going to find a woman who had disappeared in Spring and never left?

"Come with me," the Spring Maiden said. She strode into the shadows of the castle's interior, leaving them with only one option.

Follow her.

Freya tried very hard to keep her mouth closed as they walked past countless magical paintings with inhabitants that moved. The floors were a carpet of thick moss and the walls were covered with a hundred flowers, all dripping nectar on the floor. The colors were so bright here, in contrast to the Winter Court, which was filled with only shades of blue. The Spring Court was a rainbow of color, sight, and sound.

"Lovely, isn't it?" Eldridge murmured. "Most faeries spend their childhood here."

"I had no idea there was even a castle," Freya replied. "It seemed like there was nothing but gardens when I was last here."

He nodded, then pointed to a painting above them. This one appeared to be a map depicting a large country with various towns and a capital in the center. "That is the Spring Court. I know it seems like most of the courts are a small portion of an entire kingdom, but most of them are extremely large. Spring is by far the largest. It acquired more and more land as the younger faeries wanted to spend their youth in Spring."

"Wow," she whispered. The word echoed through the hallway. "It's beautiful, but I didn't know so many people lived here. I thought..."

At her hesitation, he filled in what she was going to say. "You thought you saw all of this court when you were here."

"Yes, I suppose I did."

"There's so many more surprises for you to see," he replied with a chuckle. "I think you're going to love seeing just how beautiful the Spring Court can be."

Or she would hate it. This place wasn't exactly in her fondest of memories.

The Spring Maiden stopped in an archway created by blue-bells dripping from a trellis. "Shall we? I don't think I can explain what's going on better than I can show you, I'm afraid."

Eldridge lifted a brow. "Then by all means. I must admit, I'm curious what has you all worked up, Dahlia."

"The worst thing that's happened to this kingdom." The shadows under her eyes deepened to a dark purple. "I've spent every waking hour trying to fix this, and yet... This is out of my league. I'm glad you came, because I didn't think you would. And then the Spring Court would be alone in this matter."

Frowning, Freya trailed Eldridge as he rushed into the room beyond.

Green ivy climbed up the walls to the ceiling. Bright light speared through their leaves, suggesting there was no covering above their head except plants. Moss covered in morning dew cushioned her feet. They approached a large wooden crate in the center of the room.

"It's in there," the Spring Maiden said. "At least, the proof of what I'm going to tell you is in there."

Eldridge cleared his throat. "Well, this is all rather ominous. Do I want to look in the crate or not?"

"It is ominous." The Spring Maiden walked over to the crate and threw the lid open. "Someone is hunting pixies in this king-dom, and I don't know who. They're growing more and more angry with me for not controlling this threat, but I can't even guess what would do this to a faerie capable of protecting themselves."

Freya tried to believe that she had a strong stomach. She wanted to be the powerful, brave woman who could look at what was in that crate with a calculating eye that searched for clues.

Instead, all she managed was a faint gag when she peered inside the crate.

The pair of wings were still bloodied at the ends where

someone had ripped them off a pixie. The nubs were still shim-
mery with magic, but without the powerful beat of a pixie
attached.

Heavens above, what could do that to a pixie?

Freya spun around, putting her back to the sight and
squeezing her eyes shut.

"Horrible, isn't it?" the Spring Maiden murmured. "I keep
getting pieces shipped to me from all over the kingdom. Not
from the killer, mind you. Just other pixies sending me whatever
is left of their loved ones in the hopes I might be able to find the
rest of them."

Freya heard the crate lid being shut, and only then did she
turn back around.

Eldridge couldn't seem to tear his eyes away from the crate.
His breathing was ragged, shoulders moving with the emotion
that poured through him. "How long has this been happening?"

"A few months now." The Spring Maiden's lip curled as she
too looked down at the crate. "The remains are entirely useless.
My magic is bound to the living. I can't use pieces of dead things
to find any clues, and I'm afraid my hands are tied. I've been
struggling to find the murderer, and we are running out of time."

"How many?" Freya asked. "How many have already fallen to
whatever monster plagues you?"

"Fifty two."

The horrific number rolled through her mind. Freya pressed
a hand to her mouth. "So many."

"And there will be even more if we don't stop this monster
soon." The Spring Maiden watched Eldridge with hope in her
eyes. "Goblin King, we need you. And I understand we may have
a mutual need for each other. If you help me find this killer, then
I will help you find Freya's mother. You have my word. The first
thing I do afterward will be to locate the human in this realm.
Do we have a deal?"

Eldridge looked at Freya first. There wasn't another option.

She couldn't trade all those pixie lives to rush finding her mother.

She nodded.

"You have a deal, Spring Maiden." He crossed his arms over his chest. "We'll find your killer."

CHAPTER 6

The Spring Maiden gave them their own room. She watched them with a sly smile on her face and a quirked lip as she brought them through the halls of her castle.

"You two will be very comfortable here," she said. "And now that I know the Goblin King has a consort, I will make sure to provide as much privacy as the two of you require. I know how difficult it is to find alone time when you are with the king."

Freya didn't want to even guess what the woman was hinting. If she had previously been a consort, for Eldridge or for another Goblin King, that could stay in the past. The last thing she needed was to feel uncomfortable comparing herself to a faerie woman who looked like she was made of silk.

The door closed behind the Spring Maiden, and Freya tried to take in the gilded beauty of the room.

All the greenery on the walls and ceiling was made of poured gold. The leaves that tangled up the posts of the bed, the flowers on the ceiling, even the floor, were metal. And Eldridge walked over it all like it was nothing special. As if he'd seen a room like this a thousand times before in his life.

Maybe he had. But Freya hadn't.

She was afraid to touch the small vanity in the corner with its mirror that reflected her own horrified expression back. She didn't want to even think about the fingerprints she'd leave on the giant chest in the back of the room that she was certain they had to put their clothing in.

What could she touch? Anything at all?

Even the bed looked like she would ruin it if she dared place her grubby fingers on the posts. Or the headboard. Or the footboard, for that matter.

"Why do you look like you swallowed something awful?" Eldridge asked with a chuckle.

"This room... It's... It's..." She struggled for the right word. Exquisite wasn't enough. Magnificent was too plain. There wasn't really a word to describe how this room made her feel, or the tangled knot in her stomach that she was going to break something worth more than everything she owned.

Eldridge walked up to her and cupped her face in his hands. "It's just like any other room in this castle. She didn't give us anything special, and no, you won't break anything. You aren't so strong that you could bend gold, Freya."

"But what if I scratch it, then? I could do some damage, and the Spring Maiden is terrifying." Those sharp teeth could pull out Freya's throat, and then where would she be?

Probably back in the dreaming realm with no control over her life. And that would mean her mother would remain wherever she was, lost for good. Esther would at least have Lux, but that wasn't going anywhere fast. Her sister and the goblin boy were fighting when she'd left, and Freya hadn't taken that as seriously as she should have. If she had known the Spring Maiden was going to kidnap her again, she would have tried to help mend her sister's relationship.

"Freya." His soft voice broke through her panic. "You're spiraling, and I need you to focus. We have to find a killer, remember?"

Some of the panicked fog in her mind disappeared. A killer.

Yes, they were supposed to find a murderer who was sending bits and pieces of his victims back to the Spring Maiden. In crates.

She shook her head and squeezed her eyes shut. "I don't know the first thing about tracking down a murderer. I can win in a battle of wits, sometimes. But a murderer? What am I supposed to do to help, Eldridge?"

"I suppose we'll just have to think like the killer. Why would anyone want to kill pixies?"

She had a few opinions on that. Because they were terrifying little things full of vibrating magic that liked to put people to sleep so they could watch their memories? It was all a horrible practice. Any manner of person might have disagreed and wanted to stop them.

All of that and more, really. She opened her eyes again and was yet again overwhelmed by the value of everything surrounding them. A single leaf from the bedpost would have fed so many people in her village. And here? The faeries thought this was normal decoration.

How far had she come in her life? It was hard to say. Freya still wasn't used to this place or these people, and nothing in this room was hers. Yet she still felt as though she had stepped into a life far better than her last.

Eldridge moved in front of her line of sight again. "I don't think we'll be able to think much in this room. Why don't we get some rest? What do you think?"

"Yes, I guess I'm tired." But she wasn't. Not really. Freya was so afraid to fall asleep again in this place. She didn't know if she'd ever wake up again.

They got ready for bed, and Eldridge yanked some of the pillows off the bed to sleep on the floor. Though he had claimed they were a couple to this entire court, they still weren't that close. Not yet, at least. But she had hopes that someday they would be.

Maybe.

Freya willed herself to sleep, but couldn't manage a single

moment of it. Every time she drifted off, her mind would snap back awake with the fear that she had returned to the dreaming realm and would never wake back up again.

She spent most of their "night" staring at the ceiling, waiting for Eldridge to wake. He didn't snore, at least. That was a small blessing.

The hours passed while she relived all her memories in this dark place. How she had felt so weak and afraid here. How the Spring Maiden had enjoyed her weakness, even controlled it by forcing Freya to go to parties like a doll she controlled. Freya had seen an illusion. The pixies saw reality and laughed at the weak mortal.

And yet, after all that had happened, she had returned. Now she was here helping the very people who had made her life so difficult. Who had caused her so much suffering.

She supposed that was only right, though. She should help these people because they needed it. Even if they were evil to their very core.

Eldridge eventually stretched his arms over his head and winced, moving his head from side to side. "I haven't slept on the floor since I was a child. I forgot how uncomfortable it was."

"We could always ask them to bring us a second bed," she said. Her tone was a little too hopeful, and she feared Eldridge would hear the exaggeration in her words. She wanted to get out of this place, and the night by herself overthinking everything hadn't helped.

He narrowed his eyes, then sighed. "You can't think when you're in this room, can you?"

If she spoke, she would cry. Freya simply nodded her head while holding her eyes a little too wide.

He rolled onto his feet and held out his hand for her to take. "Get out of bed, then. No one should be awake just yet. We can get some air and clear our heads. How does that sound?"

It sounded like he was taking care of her, and Freya didn't know what to do with that. He was the trickster. The manipulative Goblin King who got her into the most ridiculous of situations, but always found his way out with wit and charm.

He wasn't supposed to be the kind hearted man who wanted to make her more comfortable.

But maybe she liked this version of him. He seemed like someone she could get along with. And less like someone that required her guard to be up at all times.

Hesitantly, Freya reached out and put her hand in his. "I could use some fresh air. Maybe that will clear my mind."

"She taught you that was necessary in this place, didn't she? Fresh air was the only safety." The shadows in his eyes were a little too familiar. Freya had known it would be hard for him to be here too, but she had never learned what happened to him in the Spring Court.

He had dove head first into his disguise, and perhaps he regretted that choice. She knew better than to pick at old wounds, however, when he wanted to take her away from all this.

Freya allowed Eldridge to draw her through the gilded halls with their white marble floors. Plants dripped from the ceiling, coiled through the windows, entirely unkept and wild in their growth.

It was as if the Spring Maiden wanted everyone to see the groomed gardens and think she was well put together. But her home revealed the madness within.

They exited the castle out a small servant's door and burst into a wild tangle of lavender tails and blood-red poppies. Eldridge threw his head back and filled his lungs with clean, crisp air.

"Ah," he said on an exhale. "Now that does feel better, doesn't it?"

It did. She could think easier out here, whether that was a spell in the air within the castle, or just her own memories tainting her lungs. Either way, she was grateful to no longer be in that golden room. "This is much better."

He held out his arm like a gentleman in a fairytale. Or at

least one of the stories her mother used to tell her when she was just a babe. "Walk with me?"

There wasn't a reason in the world she would ever say no.

She linked their arms and together they moved through the lavender field. She imagined the Spring Maiden would have had a fit seeing them trudge through her gardens like this. They didn't stick to the path. They walked wherever their hearts decided they wanted to.

This sort of freedom was what she had needed in this place. Freya glanced around, still expecting some pixie to wander into view. But no one disturbed their stroll or even rustled the hedges.

"Why aren't there any pixies here right now?" she asked.

"They all sleep. There is no night surrounding the Spring Maiden's castle, so it always seems like its day here. But they sleep just like mortals." His bicep clenched. "The guards watch over them. In all the two weeks I was here, I never saw a guard sleep."

"Surely they must sleep, though," Freya replied. "It would be impossible for them to not."

"Perhaps they sleep standing up," he muttered. Eldridge's spine stiffened at the thought. "I know I used to lean against a wall to get some form of rest. Whatever they do, they aren't treated like they're alive here. To the Spring Maiden, her guards are statues animated only for her purposes. No thoughts. No dreams."

The thought was deeply unsettling. Freya licked her lips and had to ask, "Are they pixies or mortals?"

He shook his head and helped her over a particularly muddy spot filled with lavender bulbs. "I don't know. They never take off their masks, but they also don't have wings. Mortal, perhaps, or other faeries from the courts. There's no way to know who or what they were, and that's been bothering me since we returned."

She frowned and let the topic drop. The guards were another

detail they needed to fix in this court, but there were more pressing matters at hand.

Her mother needed to be found.

They had to unmask a murderer.

Why couldn't anything in the faerie courts be easy? Of course, she had been sitting in the Goblin King's home waiting for an adventure. She just hadn't bargained for the one that would be quite so... well... urgent.

Blowing out a breath at a wayward strand of hair, she pointed at a pavilion on the horizon. "What about there? I wouldn't mind stopping for a bit and getting out of the sun."

"Why would you want to get out of the sun?" He tilted his head to the side. "It feels good, doesn't it?"

"Yes, but if I stay in it for too long, then I will get even more freckles." She gestured to her face and then to her arms.

"I think your freckles are lovely." Eldridge wrapped his arm around her waist and tugged her closer. The warmth from his body was searing, and the strength in his arm was like an iron band. "I wouldn't mind spending the afternoon counting them. How many do you think there are?"

"Quite a few," she planted her hands on his chest and gave a little shove. "We're supposed to be finding a killer, Eldridge."

"Indeed." He leaned down and dragged his nose up the length of her neck. He stopped right at her ear, gently biting the lobe. "But I think we have a few moments to ourselves. After all, the Spring Maiden did say she wanted to give us some privacy. And I haven't seen this side of you in a very long time. I'm intrigued, hero of mine."

All the breath in her lungs stuttered. She couldn't quite inhale all the way, and the tiny panting sounds she was making were embarrassing. "Intrigued by what?"

"You." He scooped her up in his arms and raced toward the pavilion.

Her stomach bounced against his shoulder, but she couldn't stop laughing long enough to tell him it was uncomfortable.

Freya slapped her palms to his back, giggles bubbling from her lips and filling the clearing with the sound of joy. He didn't slow down for a minute until he placed her on her feet in the pergola.

Thankfully, there were no dreamers in this one. There was a smaller bed in the corner with silk sheets and white roses above it. Petals fell like rain from above their head.

Freya was breathless. A few more giggles escaped her mouth, and she pressed a hand to her lips to contain them.

"Oh, don't do that," Eldridge murmured. He took her wrist and pulled it away from her face. "I love the sound of your laugh."

Her heart skipped a beat. He hadn't said he loved her, and she doubted he ever would. That was a ridiculous fantasy of a young woman who had grown up hearing about faeries. But the words were so close. They were so close to saying that he loved her, or making some other wonderful declaration, and her heart thudded against her ribs.

"Eldridge," she whispered.

He stroked his thumb over the high peaks of her cheekbones. His eyes watched his hands as they moved, as though he couldn't get enough of looking at her. As though he thought she was beautiful.

And in that moment, she felt like she was.

Freya let her eyes drift shut as he held her. Even if he never said he loved her, at least she could enjoy his touch. She languished in the addicting allure of the Goblin King's attention that he gave to no one else but her.

For now.

She waited for the kiss, but he didn't lean any closer. Freya didn't feel the fan of his breath or the warmth of his lips close to hers. She grew tired of his teasing.

Patience worn thin, she snapped her eyes open, ready for another battle of wits. Except Eldridge wasn't teasing her. He wasn't even moving. His entire body was frozen exactly where he had been, eyes not moving, chest still as if there were no breath left inside him.

It was as if time had stopped.

"Eldridge?" she whispered.

Freya wiggled out of his grasp, then shoved his shoulder hard. "Why aren't you moving?" she asked. "What magic is this?"

A faint growl erupted from the bush beyond the pavilion. The sound was deep and haunting, too rough to be a pixie and not like anything she'd ever heard in the faerie realm. But she'd heard the sound back home before.

The memory was buried deep in her subconscious, but the sound made it come roaring back. She had been a little girl. Her mother was waiting for their father to return from the market, where he had been intent on buying a new hammer and tools to patch their leaky roof. The growl had been a wolf, her mother claimed. A lone wolf in the forest looking for something to eat.

They had remained locked in their cabin, shivering in the shadows, until her father returned. Her mother had shouted out the window that there was a wolf, and he'd thundered into their home with wild eyes. Her father had taken his shotgun outside for hours, searching for the beast, but he never found it.

Now, she had to wonder if the monster had been a faerie creature.

Heart pounding, she stepped around Eldridge's frozen figure and walked to the edge of the pavilion. There, just beyond the hedges nearest to her, the leaves rustled. Movement of some beast that was large enough to shake the entire hedge.

And as she watched, twin red eyes appeared through the green. They met her gaze from the shadows.

CHAPTER 7

Any rational person would have stayed with Eldridge. She should have cowered beside the Goblin King and hoped the wolf couldn't come into the pavilion because this space was protected by the Spring Maiden's magic.

Freya found herself to be less and less rational the longer she was in the faerie realm.

The wolf took off through the hedges and Freya's stomach twisted in worry. She'd never heard of a creature like this in the faerie realms. She would have heard the fae talking about the beasts. Wolves were dangerous, and they were always meddling with sheep or chickens. At least, they did in her village.

The faeries had to eat. They must have farms and livestock that they used to put food on their tables. The wolves around here must have hunted those beasts, but no one talked about them.

Or...

She shuddered to think this beast had come in from her realm and was now running rampant through the faerie realm. What if this was the pixie killer? A wolf was just a wolf. Freya had seen the men from her village hunt down packs before when they were too unruly and were getting too brave. If a wolf was what plagued the Spring Court, then that was something she could work with.

Eldridge was a warrior. He should be able to hunt down a single wolf and ensure it killed no more pixies. This would be easy if a wolf was their problem.

Except, she didn't know how time had stopped. She could easily dismiss such a thing as the magic of the court affecting Eldridge. But why wouldn't it also freeze Freya where she stood? It should have been the other way around.

If the beast was magical and that was how it hunted its prey, then she would need proof. Freya didn't care that the wolf might have hurt someone, or even that it was always a threat regardless of that death. She wouldn't kill an innocent animal without proof.

Quickly, she walked over to Eldridge's frozen form and tapped his face. "Are you going to wake up? If you don't, I'm going to do something very foolish on my own."

He didn't move.

"I'm going to take that as relenting that I should absolutely follow that wolf and report back when I figure out what's going on." She patted his face one last time and then headed out. "Good talk, Eldridge. I'll let you know what I find out."

She was quite certain that if he was awake, he would yell at her to stop what she was doing and get back here.

But he wasn't. She hiked up her skirts, hopped over the hedge, and took off in the direction the wolf had gone. The traveling gown was rather uncomfortable to run in, and she'd need to talk with Eldridge about that. If they were going to be running off into the wilds, then she needed to be wearing pants. Like him.

As it was, the brambles tugged at her clothing. She pulled her skirt from their grip with a rough tug, and the fabric ripped at the edges.

The wolf had gone into a section of the Spring Court she'd never seen before. Although, she supposed she really hadn't seen much of the Spring Court at all. The gardens gave way to the wild and unknown.

All the plants turned into recognizable bushes. Thorns, brambles, fallen branches of trees that had seen better days. This wasn't the kind of greenery she was used to from the Spring Maiden.

And it was all so close to the gardens. That was the most confusing part.

Freya reached up and knocked a branch out of her way. The branch was covered in moss, but had been snapped by a careless hand. Or a beast that had passed here before her.

She slowed her wild rush to catch up with the animal and searched the ground for signs it had been here before her. And there, in the mud at her feet, was a large padded footprint. Except... Well, it didn't look right.

Freya crouched down to get a closer look. Holding her hand next to it in the mud, she blew out a long breath at the size. "You're a big beast, aren't you?"

The sight of a wolf's footprint that was larger than her hand unsettled her. The thought that this was a wolf who had escaped into the faerie realm slowly dissolved. She wasn't dealing with a wolf from the mortal realm.

This was something different.

She swallowed hard, realizing she'd put herself in a rather precarious position. If the wolf's feet were this large, then she didn't stand a chance if it found her first. Likely she could climb a tree, but would she be fast enough to get away?

Right. She needed to think things through before she ran off into a faerie forest. Maybe she'd gotten a little too excited.

But she was in it, now. And if this fae beast was going back to its home or hovel, then she stood a chance at figuring out if this was the faerie killer. Freya couldn't stop now, even if she was much more afraid than before.

Picking her way carefully this time, she walked through the forest while following the giant footsteps. The beast had slowed. The prints were much closer together and easier to find.

She had to dodge between hedges and branches, but eventually she found herself on something like a path. An animal path, certainly, but she had walked on these in the forest where she lived before. Usually deer made them. Not this path, however, considering the amount of paw prints that padded through the mud and tamped down the earth.

Light appeared at the end of this strange tunnel made of thorns and arched branches. She slowed down, hesitating to enter the clearing beyond. What if the beast was waiting for her to step out? Wolves had incredible noses. The beast might have smelled her already, and she had no weapon.

Leaning down, she tugged at a large root near her foot. The blunt stick wouldn't do much, but it made her feel better to hold some kind of club in her hand. Just in case.

Getting onto her hands and knees, she crawled through the mud to the very edge of the path. There, she peered through the grass at the clearing beyond and sent up a silent prayer that she wouldn't meet that horrifying red gaze again.

But the beast wasn't in the clearing beyond.

The grass was classically emerald green, almost painfully vivid. Why would it be so lush when the rest of the forest hadn't been? Tiny white flowers dotted through the field, and from the back corner a lovely pixie woman emerged.

She wore a pale white dress, her wings fluttering behind her as she landed in the field. She held a woven basket in her hands, clearly intending on gathering something that grew in the field.

Perhaps that was why the Spring Maiden's magic grew in this field.

Curious, Freya lifted up onto her elbows. That was when the scent hit her. It was too much like the perfume the Spring Maiden had used to keep Freya under her spell. Though, there was no magic tainted with the scent this time.

Was this where the Spring Maiden grew the ingredients to

keep the dreamers in their deep sleep? It would make sense, in a strange way. But Freya hadn't ever thought to see this place for herself.

It was hidden. Completely and utterly hidden from any eyes that might have accidentally found it.

So this was where it all started. The pixie leaned down and started plucking the white flowers, then placing them in the basket she held. She hummed under her breath and Freya watched the shadows for the wolf.

She should get out of this path and tell the pixie it wasn't safe. The wolf might not be the one who was hunting them down, but the beast was still dangerous.

Freya didn't get the chance to warn the other woman.

The dark furred form charged out of the forest directly at the pixie. And Freya wanted to shout a warning. She wanted to scream for the pixie to fly, but nothing came out of her mouth other than a faint squeak as she flattened herself to the ground once again.

The wolf's jaws flashed in the morning light. Gleaming white fangs caught one of the pixie's wings and ripped it off before she could even think about flying. The woman let out a cry of pain and anguish, reaching for the wound that flashed bright red.

Then the wolf disappeared.

It was gone as quickly as it came. The pixie stumbled, falling onto one knee as her eyes widened with shock.

The faerie wasn't so weak, however. She bared her teeth and lifted her hands, ready for another strike. Freya tried to get up again to help, only to drop again when she heard the angry snarl.

The wolf appeared from the opposite side of the field. It was so fast that the beast moved in a blur. One moment it was in the back corner of the clearing, and then suddenly it was upon the pixie again.

Those teeth flashed, sharp and too terrible for her to look at. The last wing ripped off the faerie's back with powerful jaws clamped down on the dragonfly pattern. But this time, the pixie was ready.

She whipped around with a scream of rage and raked her nails down on the wolf's back. It let out a howl that chilled Freya to the bone.

This time, the beast didn't run away. It didn't use the shadows to get the upper hand. Instead, it stayed right where the pixie was. It circled her with gnashing teeth and Freya had to look away.

She knew what was going to happen. Anyone watching would have known, but there was nothing she could do to help.

Freya had no weapons. No magic. Nothing that could save this pixie from her fate.

She didn't even have the stomach to watch.

A scream echoed through the clearing, cut off by a crunching sound that Freya would never forget. That horrible sound made her stomach roll. She squeezed her eyes shut and tried to still the beat of her heart. She had to keep her own scream locked up tight in her chest or the wolf would know she was there. Then, she would be the next victim it claimed.

When it had been quiet for too long, she opened her eyes to see what the wolf was doing.

The beast was hunched over the pixie, jaws working hard. But the moment her eyes landed on the creature, it was like it knew she was watching.

It stopped feasting and looked over its shoulder, staring into the shadows where she hid. The red eyes seemed to glow with magic and power. Freya knew this was no wolf from the mortal realms that had discovered how to plague the pixies here. No, this was a monster who had been born in this realm. A monster created to terrorize and instill fear in any who saw it.

Hands shaking, she tried to move back on the path.

But then the beast moved. It planted its paws firmly on the ground and then stood.

Shaking its shoulders back, this wolf-like monster stood as a mortal man did. Its hunched shoulders proved to be broad and commanding. The beast's hips and legs were awkward, but this wasn't like looking at Arrow stand.

This was a monster. Half man, half beast.

"A werewolf," she whispered.

Her face crumpled in fear. Her mother had told her about these legendary creatures, but even she hadn't believed they were real. A man who was bitten by such an animal would forever be enslaved by the horrifying curse that beckoned good souls to kill and devour.

The beast shook again. It straightened its spine even further, puffing out its heaving chest as it returned its attention back to the dead pixie at its feet.

It leaned down and picked up the body. Holding the limp, bloody, and broken faerie in its arms, the werewolf met her gaze.

She should run. Freya should disappear down the path and seek out Eldridge immediately. But she was frozen in place, staring at the monster as it stared back at her.

The werewolf opened its mouth wide, baring its teeth in a snarl. And then a ragged sound came from between those awful lips.

"Freya," it snarled.

Her body suddenly moved again. Freya scrambled onto her feet and bolted back down the path with fear nipping at her heels.

CHAPTER 8

She slapped branches out of her way in her wild escape from the monster in the clearing. Heart racing in her chest, lungs heaving for breath, she ran all the way back to the pavilion.

"Please be awake," she muttered as she raced to Eldridge's side. "Come on, you have to wake up. We need to go."

Freya threw herself at the Goblin King. Hands scrambling to grab whatever she could, she tugged at his form hard.

"I will not leave you," she growled. "The beast is coming and we have to go. Now! Wake up, you damned faerie man. Come on!"

Whatever spell the werewolf had cast wore off. Eldridge blinked, then lowered his hands with a frown. He stared down at his fingers, not allowing her to move him even though she was clearly distraught. "What happened?" he asked, his face furrowed in a frown. "How did you move away from me so quickly?"

"God damn it, Eldridge. I will explain later. We have to go," she shouted.

He grabbed onto her shoulders, holding her still for a moment when she would have bolted back to the castle. They needed to put more distance between themselves and that creature in the clearing. Freya had no idea if it was following her.

Stalking her.

What if she led it back to the castle?

Obviously it had a taste for pixie flesh, so that wouldn't do. She couldn't put everyone in the Spring Maiden's court at risk. Not without warning them about what was coming.

Eldridge shook her hard. "Freya, what is going on? You're shaking like a leaf!"

She hadn't realized how badly she was shaking. But there wasn't time to worry about her. They had to warn the Spring Court. They had to tell the Spring Maiden that a terrifying werewolf who stood ten feet tall was hunting down the pixies.

Out of breath and still running on adrenaline, she stammered, "We have to warn the Spring Maiden. She needs guards. An army. All the guards possible to stand watch. Because we can't stay here. We have to go back to the castle because he's coming, but I also don't want him to catch them off guard. What if we lead him to them, Eldridge?"

He shook her again. "You're not making any sense. You didn't go anywhere, Freya. What you saw must have been some kind of premonition, or... What did you see?"

She stared over his shoulder with wide, terrified eyes. Were the hedges moving? Had the werewolf shook them while it hunted her down? "I did leave, Eldridge. You were frozen in place, like someone had stopped time. And I followed the wolf, who was in the hedges. I saw him kill a pixie. He ripped her wings off like it was nothing, and then I realized it's a werewolf."

How did one explain that a mythical creature was real? How did she tell Eldridge that a creature from her own realm, the kind of monster they told stories about at night, was now plaguing the Spring Court?

Were werewolves something the fae had even heard of?

He released his hold on her shoulders and took a step back.

Eldridge shook his head at her words. "No. That's not possible. You saw a wolf, Freya. Nothing more."

"He stood up," she whispered. She pressed her shaking fingers to her mouth. "He stood up after he killed her. And then he looked me in the eye and he said my name, Eldridge."

His eyes widened in shock. Stumbling back, Eldridge sat down hard on the edge of the bed behind them. "There hasn't been a werewolf in the faerie realm for over two hundred years. No one would ever believe you."

"He could be following me. We need to go."

"He wouldn't." Brows furrowed, Eldridge clutched the edge of the mattress. "They don't go so far. The fact that he's even coming this close to the Spring Court must mean that he's starving or... I don't know. It's unusual for a werewolf to be this close to any other faerie creatures. They hate us after we hunted them down."

"I'm telling you, he looked right at me and said my name." Why had he done that? She couldn't imagine how the creature would even know who she was.

"Perhaps he worked with the Winter Princess," Eldridge murmured. "Perhaps he's hunting you, not the pixies."

Freya sank to her knees in front of Eldridge. The marble beneath her was warmed by the sun. "He didn't try to hurt me. He just said my name, holding her body like we were going to have a conversation over the corpse."

The shock wore off and Eldridge lunged forward. He wrapped both his arms around her shoulders, yanking her against his heart and holding her too close.

He pressed a kiss to the top of her head and breathed some words that she didn't understand. His hands slid down her arms, then back up. He sank his fingers into her hair, muttering more words that made little sense.

What language was he speaking?

Freya pressed her hands to his shoulders. "Eldridge, what are you doing?"

"Shh," he scolded. Then continued with his strange ritual.

Over and over he touched her shoulders, head, arms. Freya felt a faint tingle on her skin. A prickle of electricity as magic weaved over her body and through the fine threading of her clothing.

"Eldridge, are you casting a spell on me?" Her skin crawled at the thought.

He finally stopped and heaved a ragged sigh. "I have to do something. It's not much, because I don't have everything I would need for a true protection spell. But you have to have something, Freya. A werewolf is no creature to toy with. He could tear your head from your shoulders with no thought or struggle."

"I'm aware," she snarled, pulling herself from his arms. "How dare you cast a spell on me without my permission?"

He allowed her freedom from his grip, but anger turned his cheeks a dark silver. "What would you have me do? You said a werewolf was hunting you down because you so selfishly took off without any warning. I have to protect you, Freya."

"At least ask. You know I'm not comfortable with magic. You know I wouldn't want..." She rubbed at the tingling feeling still vibrating down her arms. "I don't like it. You can't cast spells on me whenever you want."

He stood up so quickly the bed screeched backward. "You are so fragile, Freya! You have no idea just how vulnerable a human is in this realm. Would you have me watch as you run around without armor or any protection at all? I cannot have you without some form of... Of..."

"Magic?" she asked. "You know that's not how I grew up. If I have to get metal armor, then I will. But I don't want to wear magic as a second skin. It's not who I am."

"Isn't it though?" Eldridge shouted the words and threw up his hands. Black shadows poured from behind him, sinking through the leaves of the plants that shriveled at the touch of his unbridled anger. "You performed magic. We both know that. I saw you do it in the Winter Palace, and I'm certain you did it while you were searching for your sister. You have as much magic as I do, and that says something."

Anger boiled underneath her skin. He knew damned well that she didn't want to talk about the strange power that ran in her veins. She didn't want to think about the implications when there was nothing she could do to figure out where she had come from or how she had gotten these powers.

"What does it say, then?" she asked, crossing her arms over her chest. "By all means, let us argue while a werewolf stalks us. Even now he's probably watching us with a grin, getting a show before his meal."

"They hunt one prey at a time," Eldridge snarled. The sound rivaled that made by the werewolf himself. "I would not put you in danger so carelessly."

"And isn't that the problem? You've taken on this role of protector when I never asked you to be one!" She threw her hands up in the air. "You claim I have magic, but that I am weak. You say I need someone to look after me, but you're the one who keeps falling under spells. I was the one awake. I took the opportunity presented, and I found the Spring Maiden's killer."

"At what cost?" Eldridge clenched his hands into fists and a blast of magic rocked through the ground. The marble beneath their feet split, cracking open to reveal ugly, tangled roots. "You could have died. If there wasn't a pixie to distract this monstrous creature, you would have been in his jaws. Not her."

Freya swallowed hard. Maybe he was right. Maybe she would have been the creature's prey instead of the pixie, but someone had to do something. She refused to believe the only option was to wait.

She was tired of waiting for everyone else to do something.

Squaring her shoulders, she clenched her jaw and met his angry gaze head on. It didn't matter that his magic was killing all the plants around them. It didn't matter that he was arguably the most powerful faerie in all the realms.

He could not talk to her like that.

"If you want to claim we are together, Eldridge, then we have to be in a partnership. You don't get to pick and choose when we are equals. Just because this moment didn't satisfy you, doesn't mean I didn't do the right thing." She planted her fists on her hips. "I will have to take risks to help you find this killer. Those risks won't always mean I will put myself in danger. But many of them will. If you want a partner, then you have to let me be one."

His eyes watched her with so much sorrow in those big, wide eyes. He hated the words coming out of her mouth. And she understood it, in a way.

Eldridge took a step closer, and the shadows merged back into him. They gathered behind him in a dark mass, standing tall and proud. He reached out a hand and tunneled it into the hair at the back of her neck. "I'm afraid, Freya," he whispered. "Afraid of losing you. Afraid of the horrible death this monster would have given you. The day I lose you will be the day I hold you in my arms until you can say goodbye in comfort. I will not see your end by clawed hands and strong jaws."

Tears built in her eyes. Her lower lip wobbled, because those gruesome words were the kindest anyone had ever said to her. "I'm not asking you to watch me die a horrible death. I'm asking you to trust me."

With a rough groan, he pulled her against his chest again. His hands glided down her back, and he pressed his lips to her hair. "I do trust you, Freya. But when you told me you had left without me... It was like someone had ripped my heart out of my chest. I am unaccustomed to fear."

"Well, you're going to get used to it." She turned her head, pressing her cheek to his chest and feeling the thundering of his heart. "I know you don't want to put me in danger. But sometimes, I'm going to have to be."

"I know that," he muttered. "I just don't like it."

She scoffed. "No one likes being in danger. Even you."

"I do, actually. I quite like the thrill of the chase. If I had seen that werewolf, I would have called out for it and run in the opposite direction." He squeezed her tighter in his arms. "But the thought of you facing down a creature like that alone? It makes my knees weak."

Freya leaned back in his arms with a grin. "I make your knees weak, Goblin King?"

He touched a finger to her chin, tilting her head back and staring down at her with a serious expression. "Every day, Freya of Woolwich. Every day."

Heart skipping a beat, she cleared her throat and replied, "We need to go warn the Spring Maiden."

"Indeed." He released her and stepped back, straightening his suit sleeves. "Shall we tell her we're hunting a werewolf?"

CHAPTER 9

They summoned the Spring Maiden immediately. Freya
and Eldridge met her in that hidden room with the
wooden crate no one had moved yet. The box was a
reminder that they still hadn't succeeded in stopping this
horrible creature.

The Spring Maiden swept into the room wearing a white
gown decorated with flowers that spilled from her hips. "What is
it? You've already found something?"

Freya licked her lips and looked at Eldridge.

He was staring at her.

Was she supposed to tell the Spring Maiden what had
happened? Damn it. She was really hoping he would take
this one.

Clenching her teeth, she tried to manage a supportive grin
but only bared her teeth in a grimace. "It's a werewolf."

The Spring Maiden's eyes widened even more than their
normal state. "Pardon me? I don't think I heard you right, girl.
Did you claim that a werewolf is hunting pixies?"

"Yes." Freya clenched her hands in her dirty skirts. "A werewolf. I saw him myself."

The Spring Maiden's tongue punched the side of her cheek. "I see."

The silence that followed was filled with shock. Freya looked over at Eldridge, who shrugged. Apparently he hadn't thought she would take the news so well, but Freya saw it as something else. This reaction suggested the Spring Maiden had known it was a werewolf.

But that couldn't be possible. No one would have allowed a monster like that to wander around their court. And Eldridge had said the faeries had killed off most of the werewolves, if not all of them.

"Were you hiding werewolves here?" Freya asked.

"No," the Spring Maiden replied. The calculating look had returned to her gaze though, and that made it hard for Freya to believe a word the woman was saying. "Why do you ask?"

"Because you don't seem all that surprised to hear it was a werewolf." Freya crossed her arms over her chest. "I saw what that creature did to the pixie in that field of flowers you use to create the perfume that controls the dreamers. It's hard for me to believe that you are unaware of what's going on. If you know whenever someone walks through your borders, surely you knew he was here?"

Eldridge watched her speak with a grin on his face and pride in his expression. It looked like the Goblin King was impressed with her.

Freya was rather impressed with herself, if she was being honest.

"Astute," the Spring Maiden said. "But you aren't correct about everything, my dear. I have not been housing the werewolves in the Spring Court since we started a killing spree, although I thought perhaps there was someone here I wasn't aware of. You see, the borders are infallible. I am not."

The Spring Maiden lifted her hands and clapped them loudly. The doors to the room opened and a small pixie was pushed between them.

He was particularly small for their kind, and pixies were already so short. His hair was cropped close to his head and his ears were larger than most. Big, black eyes stared at them with fear in his gaze. He was shivering out of his boots. The poor thing.

Eldridge took a step closer to the terrified pixie, admonishing the Spring Maiden. "Go easy on the poor thing, Dahlia. He doesn't know what's going on by the looks of it."

"I do, Your Highness." The pixie cleared his throat. "I've just never been before so much royalty before."

This was something Freya could help with. She plastered a smile on her face and walked to the pixie's side. Offering her arm, she kept the grin on her face and hoped it looked soft and kind. "I have also never been around this much royalty. Between the two of us, I think we might be able to manage them."

His eyes got even wider, if that was possible. "But you're the Queen Killer, ma'am."

Damn it. Apparently her reputation had preceded her.

With a frown, she let her arm drop to the floor and shrugged. "Well, you can't say I didn't try. Spring Maiden, why in the world did you bring this pixie to the room? Unless he's seen the were-wolf or knows where it lives, I don't think we need more proof that your people are dying."

"Oh, he has proof." The Spring Maiden sauntered over to the crate and sat down on the lid. Crossing her legs delicately, she waved at the pixie man. "Go on. Tell them what you told me."

He opened his mouth, then clamped it shut as the Maiden interrupted him with a sharp snarl.

"From the beginning, pixie. I don't want you skipping any details like you tried to do before. Show them the truth first, and then I'll let you go."

Freya still didn't know how the Spring Maiden could be so cruel to her own people. The pixies were as mishandled as the guards, now that she was seeing it all. And suddenly, she wasn't the person the Spring Maiden's hatred was directed toward. What an odd turn of events.

The pixie man shuffled his feet, before clearing his throat and beginning his tale. "All the pixies who work in the fields have heard of this beast. He takes many forms, some of them claim. A werewolf. A magician. A kindly old man with a crooked cane and a long white beard. But all of them kill pixies, because he hates the lot of us."

Eldridge frowned. "A lot of people hate pixies. There's not much to go on there."

"Well, sir, most of us know that he's hunting pixies and not any other faerie. If you cover up our wings, then he'll leave us alone." The pixie shuffled his feet. "So we figured out a way to hide our wings and thought maybe he would leave us to work. It's the only thing we could think of to save ourselves."

The Spring Maiden circled her hand in the air. "Yes, yes. We all understand that you had to do something to keep him away from you. Now turn around and show them what you've all been doing."

Freya watched the pixie wince with a strange mixture of pity and mirth. After all, most of these creatures had tormented her while she was here. They'd made it very clear that she was nothing more than a toy to them, and while she pitied the fear they felt while being hunted, she also thought they were getting what they deserved.

He reached for the hem of his shirt and pulled it up and over his head. Then he turned around and showed them the strange contraption on his back.

A small zipper ran down his spine. And Freya was certain it was a zipper. It even had a little tab at the top, just between his bright, shimmering wings.

"What does that do?" she asked, curiosity spiking at the sight.

"It keeps us hidden from the wolf, miss." The pixie reached over his shoulders and tugged the zipper down.

With a flex of his back muscles, he curled his wings in toward the zipper. Carefully, he tucked them into the hidden pocket that he'd created with magic, then he reached and zipped it back up.

The expression on his face was pinched, almost as though holding his wings like that hurt. And she could imagine it did. His skin bulged where the extra flesh had been packed in beneath it. But the wings were gone. Contained as though they had never been there in the first place.

Eldridge stepped up to the pixie man's side. "May I?" he asked.

"That's why I'm here, Your Highness. As proof that the pixies are doing whatever we can to prevent this creature from knowing what we are." The pixie squared his shoulders. "If you must touch them, then you may."

Eldridge reached for the zipper and gently pulled it down. The wings unfurled again, though they were a little crinkled in comparison to the first time the pixie had walked in the door.

Freya couldn't keep her mouth shut. She had to ask. "Does that hurt?"

"Quite a bit, miss." A muscle in the pixie's jaw jumped. "But it's better than being dead."

She supposed that was the better way to look at it. Hiding their wings like that had to cause them immense pain, however. And no one was trying to stop that pain for them. Instead, they were suffering with the hopes that someone would eventually put an end to these dark times.

It didn't settle well with her.

"So you hide your wings, that's a good first step. We're trying to hunt it down though." She hoped the words weren't too harsh, but knowing that the pixies were hiding themselves didn't help their cause. They needed more concrete evidence. "Do you have any idea where the creature hides? It has to sleep. Somewhere it has to have a den."

The pixie stepped away from Eldridge and pulled his shirt

back over his head. "The only thing I've heard is that he is seen more around the mines. That's where the zipper comes from. The faeries in that area were the ones to figure it out, you see."

Mines?

Freya hadn't realized the Spring Court was so large. Eldridge had told her that it was, but there were mines in the Spring Court? Why would they need those?

Frowning, she looked to the Goblin King for whatever information he could give her. He was staring off into the distance, contemplating the words the pixie had said. "So he probably has a cave where he lives, then. If I remember correctly, the mines are full of abandoned shafts."

"You're correct, Your Highness. There are plenty of caves and cave systems that we don't go into anymore." The pixie shivered in fear. "There's a reason we don't go in them anymore, though. I wouldn't advise to search without knowing where he is."

"Would someone there know more than you?" Eldridge took an excited step forward, a little too quickly.

The pixie flinched back as though the Goblin King was going to hit him. He held up his hands, "Yes! Yes, I'm sure they would know something. But I don't, Your Highness. I'm sorry. I'm so sorry to disappoint."

Why was the pixie reacting like that? Did the Spring Maiden hit them?

The more she discovered about this court, the less she liked the place.

The pixie man started to slink toward the door. He clearly didn't want to be here any longer than he had to, but he froze when the Spring Maiden cleared her throat.

She still sat on the crate, staring at him with aggression and anger in her eyes. "Now tell them the last part. If you don't tell them that, then I look like a liar. And you don't want me to look like a liar, do you?"

"No, mistress." He swallowed hard, the knot in his throat bobbing up and down. "The werewolf is said to have been seen with a mortal woman. Once, a long time ago, he was hunting a pixie, and she stopped him. Ever since then, he's been obsessed with finding her again."

"A mortal woman?" Freya's heart leapt into her throat. "Do you know what she looked like?"

He nodded. "Like you, miss. Dark hair, dark eyes. She was pretty, the last time people saw her."

"Who was the last person to see her?" Was her luck changing? If someone in the Spring Court had actually seen her mother, then she could start there. They might be able to find her mother after all.

She couldn't breathe through the excitement. This was her chance. Her first real clue when they had been searching for so long.

"The last person to see her lives near the mines, miss. They said they saw her confront the werewolf. She saved a pixie life all those years ago, and no one saw the werewolf for years after that. Because... well... Because..." He tugged on the collar of his shirt. "The werewolf took her, miss. He cast some spell on her and she fell asleep. He dragged her off into one of the tunnels and no one ever saw her again."

Before Freya could ask another question, the Spring Maiden interrupted them. "That'll do. Off you go."

The pixie didn't pause to see if they had more questions. He darted out of the room like they'd set him on fire.

Freya put her hand on Eldridge's arm to battle the dizzy spell that threatened to drive her to the floor. Her mother was alive. The werewolf had taken her, but her mother had to be alive. People had seen her.

"I—" She shook her head. "I can't believe it."

The Spring Maiden stood and strode up to her. She tucked a finger under Freya's chin and tilted her head back. "I keep my promises, Freya. I told you if you helped me find this monster, that I would find your mother. This is only the start."

She met that dark gaze without hesitation. "It's a damn good start. Now what do we do?"

The Spring Maiden grinned her shark-like smile. "Now we hunt."

CHAPTER 10

It took them days to figure out their next steps. The Spring Maiden wanted to send them with the appropriate amount of guards. She said it was important that they arrived in the mining town with the forces of the Spring Maiden. Otherwise, the miners might not want them anywhere near them.

Eldridge half agreed with her. He wanted the guards, but he wanted them to remain hidden at all times. That way, they could speak with the miners as if they were friends. He said he would dress as one of them. Walk through their ranks and lure the werewolf to hunt him rather than the pixies who were obviously incapable of protecting themselves.

They woke up every morning to go meet with the Spring Maiden and argue. But every day they landed on the same realization. Neither of them agreed on anything.

Freya was reminded of Lux and Arrow arguing before she went to the Winter Court. Everyone had their opinions on what should be done, but no one was willing to listen to anyone else. Was this a faerie trait? Did they all have this foolish trait of digging their heels in even when they might be wrong?

She grew tired of it on the third day and stopped Eldridge

after they had met with the Spring Maiden. "I don't think we're going to settle on anything, Eldridge."

"She'll come around. I know her very well, and I understand her argument. But I think that the Spring Maiden doesn't realize her people are afraid of her." He reached for her hand and placed it on his forearm. "I know you're worried about all this. She wasn't always this ridiculous woman who wanted to cause harm. I still see her original personality in there. We have a chance with this one, unlike the Winter Princess."

"That's not..." Freya sighed as he dragged her down the hall toward the exit they always used. "Where are you taking me?"

"I thought we could go for another walk. There's so much you haven't seen in this court yet, and I'm taking this as an opportunity to prove how lovely my home is." He grinned. "Every court is mine, really. I think you would want to see it all."

"They aren't yours," she argued. "And I think we need to talk about this more. You two can argue until you're blue in the face, but nothing is going to happen. Has anyone even gone to get that pixie I saw die?"

"I'm sure someone has." He held the door open for her and gestured for her to walk in front of him. "They wouldn't let their own stay there to rot in the sun."

"Are you sure?"

"I'm positive, Freya. Things like this take time. The pixie was right. We can't just thunder into the mines intending to hunt this terrifying beast. We'd get lost in the dark, and then the werewolf would find us. Or something worse." He gestured again for her to go, again. "Go on. I have a surprise for you."

She'd learned a long time ago that she didn't like faerie surprises.

But his eyes gleamed with happiness, and she could at least give him a chance. Eldridge was so excited. Neither of them had worn that expression on their face in a very long time. So whatever had gotten him all riled up, it had to be good.

Freya left the Spring Castle and stepped out into the gardens beyond. "Where are we going then?"

"To the right."

If he wanted her to lead, then she would. Freya walked around the corner of the castle still muttering about faeries who thought everything would work out just fine and who didn't realize that not everything could be fine if they ignored it.

"I can hear you, you know," Eldridge called out to her.

"I know you can! I was hoping you'd take something to heart."

"Maybe someday. But for now, I think it's important that you relax a bit. This wasn't meant to be all work and no play, after all."

What did he mean by that? They were here to find her mother. Of course it was work. They had to step into the role of hero and king again. Did he think they had come to the Spring Court to... what? Galavant around?

If he really believed that was why they were here, then she would turn back around and get to work on her own. She could find her own mother, now. Freya had plenty of information to get started, and the miners were more likely to talk to her than the man they knew as king.

"Eldridge," she growled.

"Just look in front of you, Freya. Faerie realms, not everything has to be so serious." He waltzed ahead of her with his hands in his pockets. The wry grin on his face challenged her to disagree with him.

But she did. Maybe she wouldn't have a little while ago, but now she had seen multiple people die. She had been the downfall of a kingdom and a queen. Though she had saved one of those, the guilt of the other would ride on her shoulders forever.

Killing someone changed a person.

Losing one's mother changed them too.

"Eldridge, look, I know you think that life can be all fun and games but—" The words stuck in her throat.

A giant glass structure stood behind him. The building appeared to be some kind of conservatory melded with a green-house. Steel rungs allowed the glass to bubble out on the sides, and a thousand different flowers bloomed inside the glass. Heat waves radiated off the edges of the building like the movement of a pixie.

"What is this place?" she asked.

He held out his arm, pointing at the strange building in the distance. "That's for us to find out. Your surprise is inside, by the way. But if you don't want to know what it is…"

"No, I do," she quickly corrected him. "I was just saying we have little time for these kinds of fun and games."

"Of course," he replied with a wide grin. "No more fun and games than necessary, Freya."

She highly doubted he was agreeing to that. Curiosity still got the better of her. She picked her way over all the plants and vines standing in their way, then reached the front door of the conservatory. Opening it blasted her with a wave of hot air that immediately made her hair frizzy from humidity. But it felt so good to feel warm.

Tilting her head back, she let the heat and sun play over her features. A smile graced her features, and she felt all the tension drain from her shoulders. "This is beautiful, Eldridge. I never would have guessed the Spring Maiden would keep a place like this in her kingdom."

"Like I said, there are a lot of secrets you don't know about." He put a hand on her hip and shoved her forward. "Keep going. There's more."

Fascinated now, she stepped into the observatory and made her way past flowers the size of her head. Everything was larger here, like it had been infused with magic to make it more impressive. She would have stood and stared at each lovely speci-men, but there was something in the middle of all this extra large greenery.

A small blue blanket with two white sheepskins laid out on it.

There was a bottle of wine waiting for her, with two tall glasses next to a basket full of bread, cheese, and what looked like a bottle of honey.

He'd planned a picnic. And here they were, ready to enjoy the afternoon with each other.

She had to work, though. Freya sighed and readied herself to argue with him. But he slipped his arms around her waist and tugged her back to his chest.

"I know the faerie realm is vast and there is so much you have yet to explore. We could get lost in a lifetime of adventure." He pressed his lips to the side of her neck. "But I am certain the greatest adventure is getting lost in you."

She melted back against him. Prettier words had never been said, and no matter how hard her mind struggled, her heart said to stay. So she did.

Freya stopped arguing. She stopped fighting for him to see that they had work to do and let herself enjoy an afternoon with an immortal creature who courted her. Freya of Woolwich. The little girl who had grown up on the edge of the forest with a mother who hated his kind.

They spent the afternoon eating and drinking in the middle of that wonderful oasis. Freya shed the outer layers of her clothing that were meant to keep her warm. He took off his jacket. If anyone had wandered into the observatory, they would have thought the two of them mad.

But they were laughing. Telling stories about their childhood and enjoying each other's company without feeling forced.

Freya laid her head in his lap, laughing so hard she could barely breathe. "So, wait! You're telling me that your greatest accomplishment growing up was stealing the whiskers of a visiting noble?"

He coughed into his wine glass, his own gusting laughter choking him. "Yes, that's exactly what I'm saying. I snuck into his room in the middle of the night, used scissors to snip them all off his face, and then ran as fast as I could. I still have them somewhere."

"That's disgusting!" she said, trying to stop giggling but incapable of doing so. "I have no idea why you would keep those. They're whiskers!"

"They're trophies of war."

She gave him a censoring glance, although her eyes still crinkled with mirth. "He told you not to climb the curtains while he and your father were having a business meeting."

"And he should have known that a goblin boy would not stand for such a ridiculous request." Eldridge drank deeply from his wine glass, then snorted into it again. "You can't tell me you weren't a wild child, as well. You must have played pranks on your family or friends."

She shook her head. "No, not really. I was a very serious child. Esther was the one to run wild and terrorize my parents. She was the funny one. I was supposed to be the big sister and take care of her. No matter what."

"That's a shame." He brushed his fingers through her hair, smoothing each strand behind her ear and lingering once he got them settled. "But if a serious childhood is what brought you to me, then I suppose I cannot be so angry at your parents."

Her cheeks burned. "Eldridge."

"What? Am I not allowed to admire your beauty? Your strength?" He lifted a brow. "You know that I'm interested in you, Freya. More than I could ever say. I haven't felt like this before."

She shouldn't encourage him, but she wanted to know. "Like what? What are you feeling?"

He took a deep breath, expression serious and grave. With a gentle touch, Eldridge traced the barest tips of his fingers along her arm. He wrapped his long fingers around her wrist and lifted it up. Gently, ever so gently, he curled her fingers in his and pressed their hands to his heart. "I couldn't put a name to it if I tried. All I know is that this feeling is vast and deep. It is ancient and powerful, and I can hardly contain it in my fragile body. When I see you, I am both light as air and heavy as stone."

Oh, and what words those were.

I'm falling in love with you, she thought.

Freya couldn't say the words, yet. Instead, she pressed her lips together and held them in. Hoping her flesh could contain the feeling that fluttered in her chest.

Eldridge followed the line of her brow to her temple and then trailed his pointed nails into her hair. "I have no expectations, Freya. I'm merely telling you what is in my soul."

"I know," she whispered. "I'm glad we got this time with each other. Alone."

He grinned, leaned down, and pressed his lips to hers. "As am I, my hero. As am I."

CHAPTER 11

Another week flew by and yet again, nothing changed. Freya grew tired of inaction and arguments.

Yes, she understood that there was a large amount of tension in the air. The pixies were a secretive sort, and the Spring Maiden was the worst of them. Some part of that unnatural woman didn't want them in her mines.

The longer she thought about it, the more Freya was certain she had figured it out. The Spring Maiden put up a front at the entrance to her kingdom. She wanted people to believe this place was beautiful, manicured, so no one could ever question how lovely it was. The inhabitants of the Spring Court were meant to reflect that.

But the reality of this place was much darker. Though there was of course beauty, there was also a lot of darkness.

Perhaps the Spring Maiden disliked that truth because the kingdom was a bitter reflection of her own soul.

Whatever the reason, Eldridge wouldn't convince this terrifying woman that they needed to go to the mines without guards. And the Spring Maiden wouldn't convince Eldridge that he needed more information before he charged into a werewolf den. Yet again, two faerie leaders had locked horns and neither would let go.

After a week of that nonsense, she was quite done. Freya enlisted the help of a few pixies, who were a little hesitant to help until she told them her plan. After that, they were quite pleased to go about and gather all the things she needed.

Freya would not run into the darkness head first. She wasn't trying to get around either of the leaders in secret. She merely wanted to know what they were up against, how to beat the creature, and then maybe she could move forward with confidence. With or without the faerie rulers.

The pixies were pleased with her plan. One of them even smiled at her and whispered, "This is how she killed the Queen. It must be!"

And though the words made her flinch, at least it meant they had some faith in her.

Half of another week passed before everything was finally ready. Freya stepped into the courtyard where a large cart rolled into view. It was stacked high with mounds of books that apparently would give her the appropriate information on werewolves in the faerie realms.

Freya knew the very first way to solve a problem was to search for a solution within the pages of a book.

"Is this everything?" she called out, approaching the cart with her hands behind her back. Her pale pink skirts swished around her legs, the bodice hugging tight to her curves. And though her arms were bare, the sun warmed her skin to a lovely shade of peaches and cream.

"It is, miss." The pixie at the front pulled the horses to a stop, then hopped off his twisted metal seat. "Every book we could find that was related to werewolves. It'll take you a while to get through all of them."

Freya could hear a faint rustling within the books. One of the stacks toppled over, and a small snout appeared over the lip of a navy colored book. That snout belonged to a rather handsome black and white dog who stepped down off the cart while standing on his back legs. He wore a fine red, pressed velvet suit with a white collar popped around his jaw. Dashing, really, if it had been on anyone but a dog.

Arrow used his paw to shift the page of the book he held in his grip, eyes still on the pages. "Yes, I'm certain it would take her a rather long time. These books are drier than the desert. But thankfully, she'll have a little help."

The grin on her face almost hurt.

He was here. Finally, her dearest friend who knew how to help her through every adventure was here.

The pixie beside her stared at the goblin with his mouth dropped open. "How long have you been in the cart?"

"Long enough to hear you sing that horrible song. I thought pixies could sing?" Arrow finally looked up from his book to glare at the faerie beside her. "You have a horrible voice. There are people who can help with that, you know."

The pixie pressed a hand to his chest, and Freya burst into laughter.

"Oh, my friend." She snagged the book out of Arrow's paws and dropped to her knees to give him a hug. "I missed you so much."

He patted her shoulder with a small paw, struggling to get out of her grip already. "Yes, well. Good. You should miss me as I'm more helpful than these oafs. I've already looked through most of these books while we were careening through the forest. Not much help here, if I'm being honest."

She released him with one last squeeze. "Is that so? I was certain someone would have a story that would give us something to work with. How are we supposed to fight a werewolf if no one knows how? I thought the faeries had killed them off before."

"They did." He bared his teeth in a snarl. "But those battles were hard won, and we lost a lot of good faerie warriors in the process. No one knew how to stop the wolves, so we just... fought until they eventually died."

"That doesn't seem effective." Freya stood and dusted off her skirts. "Are we back to square one, then?"

Arrow reached into the pocket of his vest and brandished a very small book about the size of her palm. "Of course we're not. Square one would suggest we have no books that might help us. This one will. No one in the kingdom would have such knowledge. Other than me. Of course."

Her eyes widened and her heart stuttered. "What do you have there, Arrow?"

"My father was a collector, of sorts. He liked to know what the other creatures were doing, and thoughts about their existence. Before all the werewolves died out, he found one that was dying. Promised he wouldn't sell the secrets, however..." Arrow waved the book. "This will give you more information on how to communicate with the beast and perhaps how to kill it. If we have to."

She pressed her hands dramatically to her chest. "My hero. What would I do without you? You are a fantastic, incredible, wonderful partner, you know that?"

"I do." He rolled his eyes, holding the book out for her to take. "And you'd be on that never ending path without me. Still. Might I remind you."

"Indeed, I would be. I owe you my life." Freya couldn't get the grin off her face. It was just so good to see him after days filled with pixies and Eldridge. Finally she was around another forward thinking individual who wasn't quite so perfect.

The doors behind her opened and a wave of warmth struck her back long before she heard his voice. It hadn't taken the Goblin King very long to realize one of his own court was in the Spring Court.

"What is Arrow doing here?" he called out. Anger made his voice a little more gruff than usual.

Right, so they were going to argue.

Freya squared her shoulders and got ready for what he was going to say to her. He wouldn't like having Arrow arrive in the Spring Court, considering Eldridge had said he didn't want to bring anyone with them. But they needed the help! And who better to help them than the goblin who had started this journey with them?

She ground her teeth and turned around. "I had a pixie inform him that we need his help."

"We don't need his help." Eldridge stopped right in front of her, teeth grinding and eyes narrowed. "We've got this handled with no one else getting involved. He has a life to live, Freya. Arrow is not your servant."

"Nor would I want him to be. He'd make a terrible servant." She reached out her hand and laid it on Arrow's shoulder. "He's here as a friend because he wants to be. And he's brought us all the information we need to understand this creature, and where to go next."

"The Spring Maiden won't let us enter the mines without her consent," he snarled. "Have you not been listening at all to our conversations? You're in the room with us, Freya!"

How dare he suggest she wasn't taking this seriously? Of course she was. They were looking for her mother, for heaven's sakes!

Freya pinched her nose and tried to calm down. Arguing had gotten them nowhere so far, and it wouldn't get them any farther. She needed to calmly and rationally explain to him her reasoning. Not shout.

Thankfully, Arrow stepped between them before she could even think of the words to convince him.

"My king," Arrow said. He bowed low for Eldridge's attention. "Freya was right to call for me. I am, after all, the same kind of species as a werewolf if you think about it. I know how to find another dog. Besides, I already brought you information that you'd need."

"Such as?" Eldridge snarled.

Freya held up the book. "A recounting of a dying werewolf, written in Arrow's father's hand."

"And..." Arrow turned around and walked back to the cart. "If you two would follow me, I think you'll find this rather interesting. I found it in your library, Eldridge. Before I left, I wanted to see if the Goblin Kingdom would have more information. It did, of course."

The confidence in this goblin dog never ceased to amaze her. Freya had to bite her lips, so she didn't grin. Arrow always knew how to convince the king to do something, even though their own relationship had started on rocky footing.

She trailed along behind the two of them and realized her heart was full again. Not because she was on an adventure, but because her family was together. Parts of it, at least. But it was so damned good to see these two working by her side.

Arrow hopped up onto the cart and sat down between a stack of crimson books and a mountain of scrolls. "This is a map of the Spring Court. Not the map that the Spring Maiden would give you, I'll make that distinction now. This is the real map."

And just like that, the curious lines between Eldridge's eyes appeared again. She recognized that expression. He was excited by the possibility of what might happen next.

Eldridge reached for a folded up parchment beside Arrow's right foot. It was the same size as a book until Eldridge unrolled it. And then it was a man's arm span wide.

"Would you look at that," Eldridge said with glee. "She would be furious to know this exists."

Arrow nodded. "I'm sure she would. But that's why it was in your castle and not in the Summer Lord's clutches. Hidden away for safekeeping, just in case something happened that a Goblin King would need to step in to take care of. I assume a werewolf hunting down pixies suits?"

"It most certainly does." Eldridge snapped the map down and met Freya's stare. "Do you know what this means?"

That they could finally get on with finding the werewolf?

That they could leave these wild gardens and actually find her mother?

Freya shrugged. "Oh, I don't know. What does it mean, Eldridge?"

He growled at her, and the sound echoed through her entire being. It wasn't a sound of anger, but one of passion and desire. She'd explore that sound later if he would let her, but for now, they had an audience and a place to go.

Eldridge folded the map back up and set it on the cart where Arrow was staring at them with a rather smug expression.

Licking his lips, the Goblin King planted his hands on his hips and stared at the two of them. "We still have to convince the Spring Maiden that we're allowed into the mines. Just by ourselves, now that we finally have a map, we can follow without the threat of getting lost."

"Why do you need her permission?" Freya asked. "I think it would be more logical that the Goblin King could go anywhere in the courts. I'll inform her that we have to return home to see my sister. She's falling in love with a goblin, you see, and that's a rather difficult thing for a mortal woman. She needs her sister by her side."

The frown on Eldridge's face was almost comical. "You know, it's rather easy to forget you can lie."

"Why's that?"

"I don't think of you as a mortal anymore," he murmured. "How strange."

Arrow snorted and rolled his eyes. "Strange indeed. I didn't miss your moon eyes. Both of you are sincerely uncomfortable to be around. Just get on with it already, would you? I already picked where we need to go."

His words snapped Freya out of the strange trance. The Goblin King's eyes were just so captivating when he stared at her like that. As if he wanted to devour her mind, body, and soul. And she'd let him if he wanted to try.

Clearing her throat, she looked back at Arrow and shook herself. "Where do you think we need to go?"

He flipped the map open again and pointed to a small symbol in the center. It was right next to a sign for the mines that stretched over half the kingdom. "The town's name is Mudgate. Everyone there has been mining for a very long time. From what I've heard, no one leaves it."

"You think they'll know about our werewolf?" she asked, leaning over the map.

"I do."

Eldridge placed his hand on her back and peered at the symbol with her. "It's a good start. If they've been mining for a long time, then they'd at least have heard the stories. We can talk with a few of the older pixies. Get a head start on the were-wolf returning to his den."

"It's a better plan than we had before." Freya looked up at Arrow and asked, "What's next?"

He snuffled, then stood up on his back legs and walked to another book. "I have more research to do. You have to go lie to the Spring Maiden. And Eldridge? Try not to mess any of this up."

CHAPTER 12

Their carriage rattled down the old road filled with potholes and deep ruts. Freya was bundled up next to Eldridge while Arrow sprawled on the opposite bench. Though he was the smallest one here, apparently he took up most of the room.

She should have known better than to allow Arrow to ride in the carriage with them.

A wheel hit a particularly large bump, then she heard the tell-tale crack of a wooden wheel. The carriage rolled precariously, then slowly dropped onto its side. She barely held onto the wall but prevented her head from cracking against the side.

They were nowhere near the town. Or at least, she didn't think they were.

She bit her lip to keep an "I told you so," in and then looked over at Eldridge. "A portal wouldn't have gotten us there any faster, huh?"

"I thought we'd want some time to catch up. It's been a while since we have talked with Arrow. Just the three of us." Eldridge gripped the lip of the window and looked for all the world as though he was entirely relaxed. Like nothing had happened.

"Eldridge. The wheel just broke," she snarled.

"Yes, it does appear that it has broken. The driver may take a while to fix it." He looked at the door behind her, the one that was currently staring almost straight up at the sky. "Perhaps we should get out of the carriage and walk the rest of the way."

"That might be the plan." She reached for Arrow and tucked him into her arms.

Very carefully, she opened up the door facing the sky and clambered out. At least she wasn't wearing one of those dreadful travel gowns, or Eldridge would have been looking right up her skirts. Instead, she'd stolen from his wardrobe and put on a pair of dark leather pants, and a white billowing shirt that looked better on her than him.

Freya placed Arrow on top of the carriage and then sat with her legs dangling into the carriage. "Are you sure you want to get out?" she asked. "It looks to me like you're enjoying yourself down there."

Eldridge reclined with half of his body still on the cushions of the seat, and the other half bracing himself. "I'm perfectly fine. But if you're in a rush, hero of mine, then perhaps you should move your legs and I'll join you in the fresh air."

"Ah, the sarcasm," she replied with a grin. "I did miss the bite."

"The bite?" He reached up and pressed a clawed hand to her calf. Squeezing tight, he stood in the broken carriage, his lips close to her ankle. "I wouldn't say my sarcasm has a bite, but there are a few things that do."

Arrow made a gagging sound behind them. "Stop. Stop it, that's more than enough. The two of you need to realize we're hunting down a killer and we don't have time for whatever it is you think you're doing. Besides, we're right next to the town."

They were?

Freya stopped looking at Eldridge and glanced around them. Shockingly, there was a town just down the road from them. Although it wasn't what she had expected from the Spring Court.

In fact, it looked downright similar to the mortal town she had come from. The buildings were rundown and old, patches on the sides creating a patchwork pattern. There were three levels of the buildings, it looked like. Railings were on some of the other levels, but most were broken and didn't appear like they would stop anyone from falling.

The road led right to the town where it stopped and split off in a spider web like pattern. The map had warned them that Mudgate would be difficult to navigate. Freya just hadn't realized how challenging it would be.

Eldridge poked his head out of the carriage, a bright grin on his face. "Ah, we are closer than I thought we were. How fortunate."

She moved aside to let him emerge into the sun. Their pixie driver was standing beside the carriage with her hands on her hips. At the sight of them leaving the carriage, she shrugged and unfurled her wings. "If you're all walking to the village, I'll head back to the court if you don't mind."

Eldridge waved her off.

If only they could fly to the town. Freya wasn't excited to walk all that way and then attempt to figure out where they were staying.

Apparently, her two companions weren't of the same mind-set. Arrow shook himself, then stood on his back legs and started toward Mudgate. Eldridge whistled as he followed the goblin dog. The damn fool.

"You two look far too happy to be doing this," she muttered, trailing after them.

"I like Mudgate," Eldridge said.

"You've been before?"

"No." He straightened the sleeves of his borrowed jacket that was a little more worn than most he would wear. "But it does look like an adventure and a half. Doesn't it? There could be robbers."

Freya furrowed her brow. "And that sounds exciting to you?"

"Immensely."

If he kept whistling, she was going to hit him. Robbers were not an exciting surprise to add to their journey. The last thing they needed was to deal with vagabonds on top of trying to stop a killer werewolf and find her mother.

Was she the only responsible person in her party?

Freya trailed after the two men and marveled at their differences. The tall, lean, Goblin King walked with a swagger that suggested his confidence had no end. Arrow, on the other hand, sometimes hopped a bit in his walk as though he were trying extremely hard to appear human, even though he never would look like one of them.

They were both so near and dear to her heart, though.

The mining village became crystal clear as they walked toward it. Upon first observation, she had thought it was empty. That was not the case. People were walking around to get wherever they needed to go. They were just sticking to the shadows, hiding from anyone who might see them.

Strange. She had thought they would at least feel safe in their own town.

She stepped closer to the two men and muttered, "Why does it feel like we're being watched?"

"Because we are," Eldridge replied. "I think it's safe to say they rarely receive strangers here."

He was most likely correct. The few pixies she could see were staring at them with wide eyes. Dirt streaked their cheeks and their brown clothing had seen better days. Everything here was in tatters. The people. The buildings. Freya could only hope the mines had seen an easier fate than the people who moved around them.

"What do we do now?" she asked under her breath.

It didn't appear that anyone was going to give them a room. The moment they stepped toward one of the pixies, the creature disappeared through a back alley that they hadn't noticed.

No one wanted to speak with the unknown, apparently.

Although she couldn't blame them if their entire life had been living in this poverty.

Arrow pressed his cold nose against the back of her hand. "I don't think it's smart for us to stay here, Miss Freya. We should look for another town nearby and then return tomorrow."

She glanced over at Eldridge, but he was looking at her to make the decision. "I don't always know what is the right choice," he said with a bemused smile. "This place is likely dangerous. I'm sure there are plenty of reasons to leave, and plenty of reasons to stay. But Arrow and I will be fine. You're the mortal."

Sure, leave it up to the human to decide their destiny. Freya blew out a frustrated breath and looked around them one last time. It really was run down. The pixies didn't want them here. Even the sky was clouded over and fog descended from the heavens as though even the sun was ashamed to look upon this place.

But they were closer than ever to finding her mother. Closer to finding out the truth.

She couldn't give that up so easily. Not when it was all within her grasp.

Freya shook her head and gestured around. "There has to be an inn somewhere, doesn't there?"

Arrow grumbled out an angry sound. "Sure, an inn. That will definitely keep us safe from the robbers and vagabonds filling the streets here. I'm sure they aren't interested in kidnapping a mortal woman and trading her for something meaningless like... Oh, I don't know. Food."

His words wouldn't get under her skin. She had known this wouldn't be easy, and of course she was aware there were dangers in this realm that were unlike anything she had dealt with before. But Freya would take the risk if it meant her mother was saved.

Eldridge stepped close to her side and placed a hand on her back. "You know I wouldn't let anyone touch you."

"I do." She smiled up at him and felt warmth bloom in her chest. For the first time, she really did believe that he would protect her with every breath in his body.

Even if he had made more mistakes than she could count, at least she knew that Eldridge was a good man to his core. He didn't want to see her injured or harmed. He'd throw his own people into the mouth of the mine itself if they tried to harm her.

Arrow chuffed another angry breath. He walked away from them, tail straight up in the air. "Nice words, Goblin King. But I don't think even you could stop a mob if these pixies decide they don't want any strangers in their mix."

They wouldn't create a mob... would they?

Freya tugged her jacket tight to her sides and stayed close as they wandered through the streets. The deeper into the mining village they went, the more she was shocked at the conditions these people lived in.

The air was filled with the acrid bite of metal and loam. Each house tilted dangerously to the side, so much so that she had to assume magic was the only thing keeping them from crumbling. Every street they walked on grew narrower until she could have reached out and touched both buildings on either side of her. Freya felt her throat closing up as claustrophobia set in. Everything was too close now. If someone wanted to attack them, then there was nowhere for any of them to go.

"Eldridge?" she whispered. "Do you think we're close to the inn yet?"

"Indeed we are." He stopped underneath a sign with a carved falcon on the front. "I do believe we've made it, Freya. Now, let's see if they have any rooms available."

Part of her hoped they didn't. Then they wouldn't have to stay in this inn that looked like it hadn't seen patrons in years. But the other part of her wanted to get this over and done with. She eyed the dirt smudged windows that were so grimy she couldn't see inside. "All right, then. If you think it's safe."

"Nothing here is safe." His expression darkened. "Arrow was right about that."

Great. Just great.

They walked into the inn and she fully expected it to be filled with smugglers and other unsavory sorts. But the interior was... well. Sad.

The bar in the back appeared abandoned. There were only a few glasses of whiskey left, but they were covered in a fine layer of dust. Three tables stood near a fireplace, but two of them were missing legs and were only standing up by luck itself. And then there was the floor, which was also fully coated with filth, dirt, and apparently some sort of slick oil because Freya had to hold her arms out at her sides so she didn't slip across the length of the floor.

Perhaps the most strange and eerie detail was that there was no one in the inn. No one at all.

Eldridge cleared his throat and called out, "Excuse me? We're looking for a room for the night!"

A bang echoed from behind the bar. Or actually, from beneath it.

The few remaining bottles rattled, and a pixie appeared from underneath the bar itself. He looked worse for wear. A thin hat on top of his head had been crushed against the side of his dark brown curls. He wore an old, dark brown suit that had seen better days. A rip over the chest might have been where a pocket once was, although one could never really know with pixies. His eyes were ringed with red and his nose was overly large, also bright red.

Why had he been under the bar? Perhaps that was where the creature had been taking a nap. However, considering the man clutched an empty bottle in his hand still, Freya thought it more likely that he had drunk himself into a stupor.

"A guest?" The pixie muttered. He rubbed his eyes with his empty fist, as if by doing so that they would suddenly disappear. When they didn't, he cleared his throat and noisily dropped the bottle. "By all the faerie realms, you're really here."

"We are." Eldridge frowned. "Is this establishment no longer open?"

"Oh, no. It's open. We just haven't had any guests since... since..." The pixie scratched his head. "Well, I can't honestly remember. It's not like a lot of people want to visit a mining village. You know?"

She could imagine that was the truth of it. Though why a mining village would even have an inn was her next question.

The young pixie was shaking as he stared at Eldridge, so she thought perhaps it would be better if she intervened. Stepping into the dim light, she smiled softly. "I assume you're the care-taker of this place. My name is Freya, what's yours?"

Hastily, the pixie man yanked his hat off his head and ducked into a low bow. "Claude, madame. Welcome to the Shrieking Falcon."

Well, at least they had a name for where they were. She'd have to pull out that map again and write down the name of the tavern so they could find it again in the winding streets. "It doesn't have to be a fancy room, Claude. We're hoping to only be here for a few nights."

Claude's bright expression diminished. His bottom lip stuck out in disappointment and he heaved a massive sigh before nodding his head in defeat. "I understand. Only a few nights. Let's see what rooms are available, shall we?"

Freya frowned in confusion. Hadn't he just said that no one had stayed in the inn for a very long time? Surely that meant all the rooms were available.

The pixie reached underneath the bar and pulled out a scroll. With an elaborate flick of his wrist, he unfurled the paper all the way to the floor. He reached into his pocket, pulled out a pair of round glasses, and popped them on his nose. "Yes, I do think there might be a few rooms ready for you. If you'd follow me this way, I'll get you all set up."

They had to trust the strange pixie, even though she wasn't sure if he owned the place or not. Freya met Eldridge's confused expression and shrugged. "I'm quite tired. Might as well see if we can rest our head here, shall we?"

He nodded, and all three of them followed the strange faerie man. Except, she realized there were no wings on Claude's back. Strange, she decided to ask him about that. It might have something to do with the werewolf they were hunting.

He shifted slightly and his suit moved. At the base of his neck was a small brass pull tab. He was hiding his wings like the other pixie had shown them. Tucked into his back even while he was hidden underneath the bar.

Freya's heart twisted in her chest. She had to help these people, just as much as she had to find her mother. Their safety, and their lives, were equally important.

"Here we are!" Claude said jauntily. He tripped and fell against the door, then pulled himself together at the last second. Tugging on the bottom of his suit jacket, he met their gaze with a grin. "I hope you'll find everything up to your standards. If you need anything, I will be in the common living area."

Freya eyed his staggering walk and sighed. "He's drunk."

"Very," Eldridge replied. He pushed open the door to their room and gestured for her to step inside ahead of him. "But at least we have a room."

"At least we have that."

She should have held her tongue. Freya's gut twisted the moment she walked through the door.

The floor was at least cleaner than downstairs, but not by much. A four poster bed in the corner was missing a post. The blankets were still crumpled at the foot of the bed where someone else had clearly slept. A fireplace in the corner was likely meant to keep them warm, but she could see even from here that soot filled the chimney so thoroughly that she wouldn't dare light a fire in fear they would set the entire place ablaze.

She looked over her shoulder at Eldridge, who chewed on his lip. "Well, this is less than satisfying."

"That's a word for it," Arrow grumbled.

Freya didn't want to leave. She was so tired, and this place was so... so...

"Awful," she said.

"But not impossible to stay in for a single night." Eldridge wrapped his arm around her shoulder and spread his fingers wide in front of them. "The hearth might be cold, but that's just a reason for all of us to snuggle a little closer together. The bed might have bugs, but we don't need a bed to be comfortable."

She lifted a brow. "Don't we need at least that?"

"Oh, mortal of little faith." He released his hold on her and winked. With his classic Goblin King flourish, he whipped off his jacket and laid it down in front of the fire. "Come, Freya. We'll all keep each other warm."

"On the floor."

"Perhaps, but it will be the best night's sleep you've had in a while." He was trying. So hard.

Freya sighed and relented. "All right. Tomorrow we'll start asking around for anyone who knows something about the wolf."

"At first light." Eldridge waited until she laid down, then arranged himself around her. Tugging her against his heart while Arrow curled up in the hollow her body made.

And though she was still tired, Freya was warm. Tomorrow they would find out all the things they needed. Tomorrow, she would take on the pixies and prove to them she was trustworthy.

But tonight, she would enjoy being safe in the arms of her Goblin King.

CHAPTER 13

Maybe she thought she was comfortable a little too soon. Freya woke long before the two goblin men. She was shivering uncontrollably and the two of them were snuggled up together like the human woman with them didn't exist.

Arrow had apparently gotten up in the middle of the night and shifted sides. Perhaps he had tucked himself against the Goblin King's back, but then Eldridge had rolled over. Now, the Goblin King was the big spoon with his arm wrapped around the goblin dog.

It was an adorable sight, and she might have taken the time to enjoy it if she wasn't shivering so hard. As it was, she was mad that they were comfortable while she was not.

Blowing into her hands, she tried to bring some life back into her fingers before standing. It had been warmer in the room below with the pixie man.

She couldn't imagine it would be dangerous to speak with him on her own. After all, no one else had been in the inn. She could talk to a faerie without having Eldridge right behind her. Couldn't she?

Freya tiptoed to the door, biting her lip and wincing with

every step. The floor creaked. One of them was going to wake up and yell at her for even thinking of leaving on her own. But they didn't. She made it to the door without issue and opened the squeaking wood.

Seriously, couldn't Claude have at least oiled the damn thing?

She closed it behind her, then listened for any movement in the room beyond. When she heard nothing, Freya assumed she was in the clear. The two of them needed to sleep, anyway. They were going to be more useful in making decisions than Freya. At least they knew something about this realm. Freya was just walking around hoping these faeries took pity on her and gave her a nugget of knowledge.

Making her way down the stairs, she walked into the front lobby of the inn. Claude was nowhere to be seen.

She had a feeling she knew where he was. And that wasn't the best of places, considering she had hoped he would take guests as a reason to be more awake.

Quietly, Freya made her way to the bar and leaned over the edge. Just as she suspected, a pixie laid on the floor with one of the last bottles of whiskey in his hand. At least this one wasn't empty like last time.

"Claude," she said.

He snorted in his sleep, curling into himself and clutching the bottle a little tighter to his chest.

"Claude," Freya said again, this time with a little more passion.

Nothing again.

She looked at the bar and stared at a glass next to her right hand. This was an inn. He must have plenty of glasses that he could fill, so it wouldn't be all that bad if she just...

Freya nudged the cup from the top of the bar. It hit the ground with a solid thunk right beside Claude's head. Surprisingly, the glass didn't break. She was impressed at the craftsmanship, at the very least.

Claude let out a tiny sound of fear, skittered backward with the bottle held against his heart, and stared up at her with wide haunted eyes. "Please, no! There's nothing here, I tell you. Nothing at all!"

She held out her hands. "No, no. I'm not going to hurt you. See? It's just me. Freya. I'm one of your guests that you let into the room earlier?"

He blinked his eyes, and eventually the panic cleared from his eyes. "Miss Freya. Madame. I am so sorry. I have bad dreams, is all. What can I do to help you?"

That kind of reaction didn't come from bad dreams. That came from a man who had suffered greatly in his life and was expecting everyone to swing at him. Freya was certain this town was rough to live in, but she hadn't expected it to be quite so brutal.

How did she make it clear that she didn't want to hurt him? She wanted a little more information on how to find the were-wolf. Of course, that might be a sore subject as well, and he was unlikely to speak about it if he was afraid of her.

Freya eyed the bottle in his hand and tried on a whim, "I couldn't sleep. I remember seeing you had alcohol and wondered if you would be willing to share."

He looked down at the bottle as well, then back at her. "People don't really drink in these parts."

"That's surprising. Considering this is a mining town, and it looks a little... down on its luck." She chose the most gentle way to say this place looked like it hadn't seen a coin in centuries. "I'd imagine most people would seek help at the bottom of a bottle."

"Most people here are miners." The tension in his shoulders relaxed. "Mining while drunk could kill you, and everyone else in the shaft with you."

"Ah." She nodded. "I understand. But I'm not a miner."

The pixie opened his mouth, a question in his eyes. Then it dawned on him what she was trying to say.

Miners might not drink, that was certain. And understand-ably so. But since Freya wasn't one of those folks, she could drink with him without putting anyone in danger. Or at least, not as much as most.

He narrowed his eyes on her and cleared his throat. "You'll have to be very plain with your reasoning, Miss Freya."

"I find it's not nearly as entertaining to drink alone as it is to drink with friends." She braced her elbow on the table and popped her chin in her hand. "My companion has plenty of money for it, if that's what you're worried about. I'm certain he wouldn't mind paying for a drink or two."

That lit a fire in Claude's eyes. He was obviously a man motivated by two singular things. Drink and money.

The knowledge of those traits made it very easy for Freya to plan out how she was going to ask him about the werewolf. He lived in the mining town. This strange faerie must know about the werewolf. Or at least the existence of someone else who did know more than just fear and superstition.

Claude reached for a new bottle of whiskey and slammed it down on the bar in front of her. "I'm afraid there's only one kind of poison here, my dear."

"That's quite all right with me. You'll find I'm not very picky about my... poison." She pointed to the tables behind them. "Shall we sit?"

"None of those chairs would hold either of our weight, I'm afraid." A glint in his eyes suggested this was a challenge. As if he didn't think someone like her would be comfortable drinking at the bar, rather than at a table.

There weren't any stools for her to sit on. Freya had never been one to shy away from a challenge, however. She heaved herself up onto the edge of the table and sat with her legs crossed. Prim and proper, but still shockingly wrong for a lady of her status.

At least, that's what she assumed he was thinking.

She gestured for a glass. "Well? Tell me about yourself, Claude. I like to hear a story when I'm drinking."

It was the right thing to say. He poured her a hefty glass and then told her his entire life story with rather impressive drama.

He had been a young pixie when he first came to this town seeking fame and fortune. The metal that made magic mirrors could be sold for as much as an entire pixie home, he claimed. But eventually the mining got to him. His lungs betrayed him, but he didn't have enough money to get back home.

That's how he ended up in the inn. He worked here for the previous owner, cleaning rooms back when the mining town had been booming. Now that there were a lot of magic mirrors, and very few people would risk breaking something that powerful, the town had died.

As did the original owner.

He spewed the story with all the flair of an actor. Freya found herself more and more captivated by the tale. Perhaps it was the drink that rushed straight to her head, but she teared up when he claimed he missed his family, but there was no way to get in touch with them.

She pressed her palm against her heart. "I would do anything for my family."

"I could tell that when you walked in the door." He hiccuped and then winced. "You're a kind hearted woman, Miss Freya. I knew that with the first look I got of you."

Those blasted tears returned again. They filled up her eyes, and she held them open frantically so she didn't start crying. "That's an awful nice thing to say."

"Well, it's the truth." Claude lifted the bottle to his lips and took a large swig.

When had they started drinking straight out of the bottle? She'd thought they were drinking out of glasses.

But when she looked down at her own hand, she wasn't holding the glass. She was also holding a bottle that was about half full of whiskey. Good lord, had she drank that much? She'd been sipping while Claude was telling his story and then... then...

Sighing, Freya put the bottle down on the bar and slid it away from herself. She needed her wits about her for this.

"Claude?" she asked. "I came here for my family, you know."

"Here?" He narrowed his eyes, trying to focus on her but looking over her shoulder. "Why would any of your family be here? This isn't a place for anyone like yourself, or even those men upstairs."

"My mother came here." Freya couldn't look him in the eye when she told this story. She needed to focus on the words, not his reaction. And for some reason, that was very difficult with so much alcohol in her system. "I don't know why, but I plan on asking her when I find her."

"For love?" Claude leaned against the bar but somehow still weaved side to side. "I know a lot of people who came here for love and then fell out of it. She could be anywhere by now. Or in another, better, part of the Spring Court."

"No, you see... The last person who saw her said she was unconscious after trying to fight a werewolf." She looked up then to meet his wide-eyed stare. "I know she's not dead. And he has her somewhere."

Claude's throat bobbed in a heavy swallow. The fear in his gaze was proof he was well aware of the beast she spoke of. He'd heard of this werewolf, and he feared it with every bone in his body.

She needed him to tell her what he knew. That determination banished some of the fog from the whiskey, enough so that she could lean forward and put her hand over his. "I think you know what I'm talking about, don't you?"

He nodded and pressed his lips together. "We all know about the werewolf, miss. That's who I thought you were when you woke me up. I was certain the shadow looming over me was the wolf come to claim my wings."

"Why your wings?"

"So we can't fly away while he's killing us, miss. Every pixie knows to be afraid of the wolf." He moved away from her and wiped the back of his hand over his mouth. "You don't want to find that creature, miss. If she went with him, then she's gone for good. You might as well give up."

Freya shook her head fiercely. "No. I will never give up on finding her."

"You have a death wish, then." He set his own bottle down and backed away from her. "Maybe you should go back to sleep. I don't think the werewolf is going to walk through those doors any time soon."

She looked over her shoulder at the solid wooden frame. The frosted windows revealed nothing that was happening on the street beyond, but she knew the danger that still lurked in the shadows. And that knowledge filled her with a sense of purpose and adventure. Unlike the pixies who lived in a constant state of fear.

"He is out there, though," she murmured. "Isn't he?"

"Not on the streets." Claude cleared his throat. "At least, I hope not. The last time he came into the town, he left a trail of carnage in his wake. Twenty five pixies all dead in their beds. No one heard him enter, and no one heard them scream. It was over in a moment of blood and pain."

The clinking of glasses caught her attention. Freya looked back to the pixie who was arranging things behind the bar. For the first time in a very long time, it looked like.

"Claude," she mumbled. "You know how you feel about seeing your family again? How you said you would do anything to get out of here and hold them in your arms?"

"It's a pipe dream. I can't see them again because I'm never getting out of here. Don't compare that to your story, Miss Freya."

She shifted closer, swinging her legs to the other side of the bar. "It's the same thing, though. I know she's out there. I know, if I tried hard enough, that I would be able to hold her in my arms. I don't care if it's a death wish to take on the werewolf. I need to find my mother. And I need your help to do that."

Claude turned away from her. He braced his hands on the edge of the shelf where most of his remaining whiskey was held. His shoulders curved in on himself and she could see his shirt moving where his wings were trying to flutter underneath the skin. "I can't help you rush to your death. That guilt would stay with me for the rest of time."

"I'm not going to die." She hopped off the bar and placed her hand on the wings slithering beneath his skin. "The man with me is the Goblin King. And the goblin dog is his faithful companion. If anyone could rid you and your people of this nightmarish monster, it is us."

Perhaps it was the alcohol loosening her lips. She was certain Eldridge wouldn't have wanted to tell the pixie who he was. At least, not yet.

But she spewed the words in the hopes they would get one step closer to her mother.

And it worked.

Claude heaved a sigh. "You need to speak to the Magician then. He's the only one who knows anything about that creature."

"How do I find him?" She tried to control the excitement in her words.

"I'll draw you a map."

CHAPTER 14

"Freya."

The words split through a headache that made her entire world spin. This was worse than when Eldridge had been forcing her mind to live through his magic. Worse than any pain she'd ever felt in her entire life.

Groaning, she put her hands to her temples and whimpered.

"Freya," again the word came. Although, this time it was at least said a little more quietly. "We were terrified when we woke up without you. What were you thinking?"

Thinking? She wasn't thinking at all through the pain in her skull. Who was talking to her, and why were they doing it so loudly?

She blinked open her eyes that felt like someone had thrown sand in them. She was face down on a wooden slab which was strange enough. But as she forced her head to raise, she realized she was also staring at an empty bottle of whiskey.

Oh.

Maybe that was why her head was hurting.

Groaning again, she eased upright and rubbed her hand on her cheek. "I don't remember."

"What do you mean, you don't remember?" Eldridge tucked

his hand underneath her chin and forced her to look at him. "Did that pixie hurt you? What spell did he cast?"

Another voice interrupted them, yet again far too loud for comfort. "That 'pixie' did nothing to her. I take offense that you'd assume I would harm a patron. She just can't hold her alcohol. The girl said she wanted to drink, and faerie realms she did. But apparently a bottle of whiskey was a little too much for her."

Yes, that was right. She had come down in the middle of the night because the Goblin King had been spooning his goblin dog. And she had wanted to talk with Claude on her own. He'd offered her whiskey and then...

Nope. Nothing. She remembered absolutely nothing from the night before.

Maybe if she could focus on something other than how the ground was moving beneath her. Was there an earthquake? It felt more like she was standing on the bow of a ship instead of the shuddering of the earth. But she was in the faerie realm. She didn't know what an earthquake would feel like here.

Eldridge sighed. "You're hungover."

"Very." She felt her stomach roll, then pressed her fist to her mouth, so she didn't spew liquid all over the Goblin King.

"Arrow and I planned to find food. I see you are in no shape to join us." He patted her head, while clearly angling his body away from her just in case she threw up. "Why don't you go back up to the room and get some rest? I'll wake you when we return."

That sounded lovely. Even if she could find a little water to splash on her face, that would be ten times better than what she was feeling right now. Freya nodded and slid off the bar. "I think I probably need that."

"Then it's a plan." He smoothed his fingers over the tousled locks of her hair. "You're a never ending surprise, Freya."

She didn't have the mental capacity to guess what that meant.

Freya staggered back to their room and stumbled to the corner where someone had placed a bowl of water. If Eldridge had already used that to clean himself this morning, then she didn't care. She needed some water on her face, immediately. Otherwise she was going to keep this grimy feeling on her body forever, and she just couldn't stand that.

She splashed the cold water on her face and let it settle the strange rolling. Her head cleared enough for her to at least think. She patted the stand the bowl sat on and realized there was no towel.

Dripping, now cold, she sighed and grabbed the end of her jacket. At least she could wipe her face with that.

Her hand hit the edges of a piece of paper tucked into her pocket.

That was strange. She didn't remember putting anything in there, but she remembered little from last night.

Blinking away the water droplets and the last remaining fog from her eyes, she tugged the piece of paper out of her pocket. It was a map of the winding streets of Mudgate. And a tiny spot marked on it which was penned, "Magician."

Strange. "Magician?" she whispered.

The sound of the word blasted her with all the memories from last night. Suddenly, she recalled the conversation with Claude and how he had been certain this Magician would know how to get her to the werewolf.

And Eldridge was out with Arrow somewhere. Damn it.

Racing from the room, she leapt down the stairs and back into the main entrance of the inn. Breathless, she slammed into the bar once again. "Claude. How long did the Goblin King and his companion say they were going to be gone?"

He looked up from his position on the floor. "They didn't say."

"Do you think it will take them a while to find food?"

He lifted the bottle to his lips, then smacked them. "Considering I didn't tell them where to find anyone who would give them the time of day? Probably until nightfall."

Damn it. That wouldn't do. She needed to find this Magician, now. Freya had never been one for patience, especially when she was holding the answer to all their questions in her hand. All she had to do was follow the line on the map. How hard could that be?

After all, she had traveled through the faerie courts on her own before. The Spring Court couldn't be that different from the others.

Pressing the map to her chest, she backed away from the bar. "I'm going out, then. Do tell the Goblin King that I'll be... busy. If he asks, just let him know I'll return. Does that sound like a plan?"

Claude lifted a hand in a salute. She could just see the tips of his fingers over the edge of the bar. "You can trust me, Miss Freya!"

Somehow, she doubted he would even remember they'd had this conversation. Eldridge would be angry with her, but... this was their chance. And she didn't want to wait.

She opened the door and charged out onto the street. Ready to take on any pixies that might step into her way or try to stop her. She was the fearless Queen Killer, and no one was going to stop her.

Freya walked into a broad chest, slamming her nose into a sharp collarbone.

"Ouch," she muttered.

Fear didn't have the opportunity to speak. She knew that chest, the apple pie scent, and the soft clothing that had only barely cushioned her nose. The Goblin King had not gone with Arrow to go get food.

"I thought you couldn't lie," she snarled, rubbing her face.

"I didn't lie." He watched her with an all knowing gaze. "I had a feeling when I left with Arrow that you weren't in your right state of mind. I decided at the last second not to go. And that I would wait outside the door just to make sure you didn't do anything stupid. Like this."

"I'm not doing anything stupid." She brandished the map at

him as though that would make this situation better. "I'm going to find someone who can help us with our werewolf problem."

"And where did you get that?" He snatched it out of her hand. "This is a dangerous part of Mudgate. You aren't going there on your own."

"Well, I planned on it." If it was dangerous, however, she was grateful he was here. Even if that meant that he had to sort of lie to protect her.

Freya was still angry he was lurking at the front door like some kind of bodyguard.

She reached for the map again, only to have him pull it out of her reach. "Eldridge. I would have been perfectly fine."

"You most certainly would not have been." He snorted. "You aren't even controlling your magic. Even though you shouldn't have any to begin with. We really need to dive into that, by the way. How do you know how to cast spells?"

"I don't," she growled. "What would you have done if I snuck out the back instead of the front door?"

"I assume you would have been deterred by the pixies who are sleeping in the back alley." He shrugged. "But if you were foolish enough to try climbing over them, I suppose I would have known where you were by the sound of your screams."

She hated that he was right. She hated that he was anywhere near close to guessing what her plans had been, and that she would have still tried to get over those pixies.

Freya jabbed her finger at him. "You don't know me so well, Goblin King. Don't get any of this twisted in your head. Just because we're..." She gestured wildly between them. "Whatever we're doing. It doesn't mean that you know me, yet. We haven't even talked about each other all that much."

He backed her against the door to the inn with an arm braced over her head. "I do know you, Freya. I know you're brave and you're thoughtful. I know you're foolish too, and that you'll stop at nothing to get your family back. Even follow a

Goblin King into the faerie realms and somehow think you might beat me."

"I know I can beat you," she whispered.

Why was he so close to her? She couldn't think about anything other than the heat of his lips and the pulse at the base of his throat. She wanted to press her mouth to the strong column of his neck, to taste him again because it felt like forever since the last time she had. It had been too long.

She cleared her throat and said, "I think we should get going if we're going to find this Magician."

"What's the hurry?"

"My mother is the hurry." She refused to believe he didn't understand that. "Claude made it very clear what kind of monster we're hunting. It's his opinion that my mother couldn't have survived this long in the werewolf's clutches."

"And yet, the Spring Maiden seems to believe she could have. She wouldn't have made a deal with us, otherwise."

Freya wasn't so certain. All the leaders of the courts did what they felt was necessary to get what they wanted. Including throwing other people into dangerous situations. Maybe the Spring Maiden didn't know if Freya's mother was alive and only assumed she was. They still might find her mother and then realize with horror that she'd been dead for a very long time.

What would that be like? She didn't think she'd survive that disappointment.

"We have to go," she repeated. "My mother might only have a few more days to live. There's no way for us to know either way, Eldridge. If this Magician can get us closer to her, then we need to take the risk now. Waiting might only make it more difficult."

He sighed and released her from the door. "Yes, fine. But I don't understand why we couldn't have waited until after breakfast."

"Because Claude didn't tell either of you where to go to get that food," she replied. "He made it very clear that you wouldn't find it without a map. Arrow won't be back until tonight."

"Excuse me?" the Goblin King exclaimed.

"You'll have to walk on an empty stomach," she said with a grin. Freya tapped her hand against Eldridge's chest and took off to follow the markings on the map. "You've done that before, haven't you?"

The streets were closer together here, and wound in a strange network of avenues placed where they needed to be. Not that it made sense to the average person. The grey stone streets, drab walls, and black soot made it seem like all the color had disappeared from the world.

Eldridge grumbled something under his breath and raced after her. "Freya!"

"What?" She glanced over her shoulder and grinned. "I know you probably haven't worked on an empty stomach before, but I think most people here have. Maybe it'll help you connect with them. What do you say?"

"I say I'd like to pick up some food along the way if we see it." He was frowning so hard his brows nearly touched.

She supposed they could do that, but doubted they would find anything suitable to the Goblin King's taste. Honestly, she could forget her grumbling stomach if they found the Magician.

Freya could only hope it would be easy to find him.

CHAPTER 15

"Freya, we have to turn right." Eldridge pointed down a dark side alley that certainly didn't look correct.

She held the map up and peered at the three streets in front of her. Something was wrong. The map said there were four offshoots here, not that there were three. The main road didn't count, it clearly said so. And turning right would only send them down the third street, not the fourth.

Frowning, she tilted the map to look at it from another direction. "I don't think we do."

"I know it might seem strange, but these streets change all the time. The map says to take a right. It doesn't matter that one of the streets is missing," he responded. Eldridge had been getting grumpier the longer they walked without getting him food.

She stored the information away for another time. Adorably, the Goblin King got angry when he didn't eat first thing in the morning. She would have to tease him about that later.

"I really think that's not the direction," she replied. "Look at this with me, would you?"

Stomping over to her side, Eldridge pointed to the map.

"Even if we were missing a street, this one would still be the correct one to go down."

But that didn't seem right. The Magician's store should be beside them. It was in the first building on the street, and it wasn't the way he wanted to go.

"This is a magician's store, Eldridge. Don't you think he might try to hide it from people?"

"Not from potential customers." He strode over to the wall where the street should have been. "What do you think I need to do? Cast some spell over here so the Magician will let us in? There's nothing here!"

Nothing but a wall with a few posters on it. She eyed the paper, mostly sketches of people who were missing. So many families hoping to find each other and praying no one was lost to the werewolf.

"I guess not," she replied. "I just thought it would be here. That's all."

"Nothing but the reminder that we are running out of time." He turned with a solemn expression. "Look at all these people. So many pixies are looking for so many lost souls."

She walked up beside him, holding the map against her heart. "Do you think they all fell at the claws of the werewolf?"

Though his eyes darkened and his jaw worked, Eldridge never replied.

Freya's heart twisted in her chest, beating hard against her ribs because her very soul knew that they had a larger purpose here. Sure, it was easy to forget when she was also trying to find her mother. But look at them all.

So many faces of so many people. Each one was sketched by loving hands, although some were more talented than others. Their eyes stared out through the pages, begging her to help them. To find them. Or, at the very least, kill the creature who tormented all the pixies in the Spring Court.

"Wait a minute," Eldridge narrowed his eyes and shifted one of the missing posters aside. "Would you look at that?"

A small mark was painted on the wall in front of them. It was the vague shape of an eye, though the iris was a spiral of color rather than an actual eyeball.

"What is it?" she asked.

"The mark of a magician," he replied with a grin. "You were right after all, Freya. There is another street. We weren't looking in the right place."

Eldridge placed his thumb in the middle of the spiral. The wall groaned, then shifted. Dirt and dust rained down on top of their heads, but the wall moved to reveal its secrets. Another street, shrouded in darkness, with small street lights lit by three candles in each.

This place wasn't so dusty or soot covered. It looked as though it had just rained on these cobblestone streets. They were slick and reflected the glimmering, warm light. There also appeared to be only one shop.

Glass windows poked out into the narrow street, warm light spilling out of them. A single sign hung above the windows with a potion bottle inscribed on it.

"Ah." Freya muttered. "A magician would hide their shop from prying eyes, I suppose."

"There are many who would like to steal the secrets of a magician. Of that I'm certain." Eldridge still wore a frown, however. "I hope he hasn't laid any traps."

"How would he sell anything if people couldn't walk down the street?" The question seemed logical, but Freya had learned a very long time ago that logic had no place in the faerie realms.

Eldridge bit his lower lip. "I'm not sure he wants to sell things, Freya. I think the only people who go to this man are the desperate and the depraved."

How quaint. And now they were here.

She wondered which category they fell into.

She wouldn't wait any longer. Taking a deep breath, she strode down the street toward the shop and hoped nothing was about to attack her. Every step echoed, as if another person were walking right beside her. Except, Eldridge didn't make any sounds at all when he walked. So that second person couldn't be him.

"What are we going to ask when we find him?" she whispered as though someone was listening to their every word.

"I would suggest we be as truthful as possible. Magicians are... difficult." Eldridge struggled to find the right descriptor. "They have a lot of magic at their fingertips, but they rarely use their magic for any reason other than satisfying their own desires. We have to make him want to help us."

Right, because that would be so easy. Can you help me find my mother, sounded like something the Magician had probably heard a thousand times before. What set Freya apart from the hundreds of pixies who had begged for the same thing?

She'd have to come up with something, and fast.

Freya paused in front of the door and licked her lips. "What are the chances of him wanting to help us out of the kindness of his own heart?"

"I would say the chances of that are zero at best."

Pressing her hand against the door, she repeated, "At best?"

"Negative chances, honestly. I wouldn't expect the Magician to be a good man at all." The warm light illuminated only one side of Eldridge's face. The other was cast in a terrifying shadow that made it seem as though he had two faces.

As if he were two people in this moment, not just one.

Shivering, she pushed the door open and entered the Magician's shop. The bell rang over her head, and she was immediately greeted with a wall of objects on shelves. Skulls, mummified creatures, gemstones that seemed to swirl with smoke. A thousand objects, all brimming with dark magic. They were terrifying and fascinating.

An orb sat on the middle shelf within eyesight. Smoke swirled within the glass, writhing and moving with some inner power that called out to Freya.

Touch me, the smoke seemed to whisper. And see what the future holds.

She couldn't do that. Nothing in here should be touched by a mortal, and yet everything was so infinitely tempting. Perhaps that was the power of the Magician. He made people give themselves up by touching some cursed object, and then he never had to deal with them at all.

Eldridge's hand came down on her wrist.

Freya snapped out of her thoughts and was horrified to see her fingers were a mere inch from touching the orb. It would have been so easy to move a little more, and then she would have answered the magical object's call.

"Don't touch that," Eldridge snapped.

"I wasn't trying to." Freya shook him off her and rubbed her wrist. "I didn't even know I was reaching for it."

"Freya..." He took a step closer to her, dropping the volume of his words until she could barely hear them. "We need to talk about your ability to use magic. A place like this is more dangerous for you if you don't know what kind of power runs through your veins."

"I do know," she replied, stepping away from the shelves. "None."

Freya walked around the wall of shelves to the interior of the shop. A cauldron bubbled in the corner, freestanding and floating in mid air. Glass vials lined the walls, filled with every type of object. Some earth. Some water. And even a few that seemed to be filled with tiny bones. She hoped the Magician had gotten those from a bird or a rat, rather than some fae creature she hadn't met yet.

And seated at a desk on the far wall was a very elderly gentleman. He had a long white beard that nearly touched his hips. Round spectacles sat on his nose and magnified his eyes, making them extra large. He wore a robe the color of the sea, and she half expected to see a pointed hat on his head.

The man was rather exactly what she had expected a magician to look like. Freya didn't trust him already.

"Ah," he said. His voice shook as he spoke. "I have been expecting you two today. Took you long enough to find the street."

"I'm afraid it wasn't very easy to find," Freya replied. "You were expecting us?"

"I don't get customers every day. But my dear Arabella let me know you would be here soon. She's never wrong, you know." He stood and rounded the desk.

The Magician used a curved cane to move around his shop. Although she wasn't certain if she could call it a shop when there didn't appear to be anything available to buy. His spine was bent in on itself, like the oldest of people she'd seen before.

In fact, he looked very much like every mortal she'd met.

Frowning, Freya looked at Eldridge with his silver skin and tufted ears, then back to the Magician. "Are you a mortal?"

The grin on the old man's face let her know that she was at least in the right line of guessing. "Mortal is a rather limiting word, don't you think? The right question, my dear, is if I'm human."

More riddles. Yet another person who wanted to talk around the truth rather than just say it.

"Well, if you're human, then you've been in the faerie realm for too long. You're already speaking in riddles, old man." Freya shouldn't have grumbled at him, but she was so tired of being treated like this. "From one human to another, I thought you'd be more helpful."

Eldridge choked behind her.

But the Magician laughed. "Such spirit! I wouldn't have expected anything else from a woman who tied herself to a Goblin King."

Maybe Eldridge didn't understand the game here. She had walked in expecting a powerful faerie creature who would tear her apart with just one look. But this man? He was a human, like her. And he probably hadn't seen one of his own kind in a very long time.

She didn't have to convince him of anything. All she had to do was give him a little taste of the world he had been missing.

Freya looked over her shoulder at Eldridge, then snorted. "And I would have expected more from a fabled Magician. You're old, sir. And yet, I'm supposed to be afraid you'll cast me down with a curse?"

Yet again, another choked sound from Eldridge erupted before he leapt in front of her. "Please don't take her up on that. We both know you're very capable of cursing us into toads. I prefer her in the form she's in. If you don't mind."

The Magician watched the Goblin King's antics with a bemused smile on his face. "Yes, I imagine you are rather fond of this form. She's a beautiful young woman. And more intelligent than you."

Freya didn't want to torment poor Eldridge much longer. She'd taken a risk in teasing the old man, but she was certain the Magician would want to be treated like he was back home. Ribbed a bit for his age. Teased by someone who was much younger, while he still held all the power in this conversation. Obviously, she wouldn't be here unless she needed something from him.

She walked around Eldridge and grinned at the Magician. "I imagine it's been a long time since you've seen another human."

"And a talented one at that." The Magician struck the floor with the end of his cane. "What is your name, miss?"

"Freya."

"Ah, what a lovely name. Your mother must have had wonderful taste." He pressed a hand to his chest. "My name is Soren. And Arabella is over there, if you have a care to meet her."

She followed the line of his finger to the Madame Arabella who had foretold their arrival.

A human head sat on a small podium in the back corner. Her

mouth was affixed open, her eyes as well. She had once been a lovely blonde with pouty lips and big blue eyes. Now, she was a frozen head who apparently spoke to the Magician whenever he wanted her to.

The reality of their situation crashed down on her head. Eldridge was right. She hadn't walked into some famed magician's workshop and wooed him because she was a mortal just like him. He was a dangerous man with more power at his fingertips than she could ever imagine.

She should treat him as such.

Gulping, she kept the smile on her face and returned her attention to the Magician. "I was hoping you could help us," she said. "We seek the wolf."

The Magician grimaced, but nodded. "Yes, I knew you were looking for that cursed beast. I thought maybe I'd get away from talking about him today. Come on, then. Have a seat and I'll get you some tea. You have questions that will take a long time to answer."

Freya didn't want to stay in this room any longer than necessary. Looking over her shoulder, she met Eldridge's wide-eyed gaze. Apparently, he was also in a rush to leave.

Unfortunately, neither of them could.

She kept the fake smile plastered on her face and said, "Tea sounds lovely."

CHAPTER 16

They sat at a table far from Arabella. Thankfully, Eldridge took the seat where the severed head remained within eyesight. Freya wasn't sure she would have been able to peel her eyes away from the macabre figure.

"He's not going to poison us, is he?" she whispered.

"I don't think so, but you were exceedingly rude to him so one can never know." Eldridge crossed his arms over his chest and glared at her. "Why can't you ever trust me? I said to woo him. Not to call him an old man incapable of magic."

"I didn't say he was incapable of magic." She didn't think. Freya could admit she'd gotten a little carried away in their banter.

It had seemed like the Magician was enjoying himself, though! How was she to know that he might get insulted? That's how he would have been treated in the mortal world. A little ribbing. Some fun jesting from a much younger woman. He had appeared to enjoy the comical moment.

Now, she wondered if it was all a big show so he could go behind the curtain near his desk and get poison to put in their tea. He was a magician, after all. No one would know where the

Goblin King and herself had gone. It wasn't like Claude would remember and tell Arrow.

They were on their own here.

Cheeks burning, she wiggled lower in her seat. "I guess we just hope it's not poison, then?"

"If we're lucky," Eldridge snarled.

The curtain flipped open and Soren came back out with a pot of tea in one hand and three teacups floating in front of him. "I'm not going to poison either of you. You're both so dramatic."

Freya rushed to help him with the cups, her chair screeching on the floor in her hurry. She snatched all three out of the air and gently set them down on the table. "You could have asked for help, you know."

The Magician smiled at her, but there was an edge in his smile that made her a little frightened. "Trust me, Miss Freya. If I needed help, I would have asked for it."

She supposed he wasn't the type of person who needed help from anyone. "Well, you have survived this long on your own in the faerie realms. I don't think I'm the one to question you on whether or not you need help."

"And don't you forget it."

Soren set the teapot on the table and took a seat with them. There was one chair left empty, and Freya had a sickly feeling that it might be for Arabella. The Magician didn't bring his head over to the table with them, but there was still a presence in that chair that she could feel.

He took a long time pouring the tea. He made sure there were enough tea leaves in each cup and set a small mesh net down afterward. It was a rather clever contraption that would save them all the bitter taste of fresh tea leaves. Once he had poured the hot water, Soren clasped his hands and sighed. "Now we can talk. I find there's less to say without a cup of tea in my hands. Don't you agree?"

She wasn't sure. Freya had never had issues talking after she'd come into this realm.

But if the Magician wanted her to drink something, then she would drink. Freya lifted the cup to her lips and blew on the hot liquid. "I suppose you're right. You know why we're here, it seems."

"Werewolves. It's all anyone talks about in Mudgate." Soren shook his head in disapproval. "I never know why. They aren't all that interesting as far as magical creatures go. Easy to track. Easy to kill."

That was reassuring to hear. Especially from this magician who was unlikely to hide details. If they were going about finding a werewolf, then he would be honest in how difficult it was.

Or at least, she hoped he wouldn't hide any important facts.

Freya sipped the scalding tea. "I'm glad he'll be easy to kill. I was expecting you to tell us that it will be much more challenging."

"In a way, it will be. You can find the wolf. You can kill the creature. It's navigating the mines that you should be the most concerned about." Soren leaned back in his chair and eyed her with a look that suggested he knew something she didn't. "And perhaps what you might find about yourself as you walk through the magic mirrors. You are a curious one, my dear."

Eldridge nodded and took his own teacup in hand. "I've told her the same thing. Walking through a magical realm without control over her own powers is dangerous."

"Indeed it is. But, considering the look on the young madame's face, I don't think we're going to have this conversation for a while yet." Soren grinned. "Am I right, Freya?"

She was about to throw her teacup at both of them. Already Freya imagined sending the scalding liquid into Eldridge's lap and knocking the old man over the head with the porcelain cup. Maybe then they would take her a little more seriously.

Her magic wasn't what they were here to talk about. And yes, she understood that there was something strange going on with her.

She'd cast a few spells in the Winter Court, and she didn't

know how she'd done them. It was almost a natural response to something she wanted, which no human should be able to say. And yet, here she was.

More confused than ever.

But she would answer those questions soon. Not here when they should use this time to find out more about the werewolf, her mother, and the terrors the pixies lived with every single day.

Instead of arguing or hitting the two of them over the head as she wanted, she lifted her teacup again and took a steadying breath of peppermint. "We're not talking about that right now. We're talking about how to find the werewolf and my mother."

"Your mother?" Soren sat up straighter, his eyes wide and his shoulders suddenly broad. "Your mother's name wasn't Astrid, was it?"

Her blood ran cold through her veins. "That was my mother's name, yes. The Spring Maiden sent us here because she thought we might be able to find her. She was last seen here. The werewolf dragged her away after she tried to save a pixie from him."

Soren's chair screeched as he stood. He tapped his fingers on his head, drumming them like he was playing the piano on his temples. "No, no, no. This isn't right. You shouldn't be here, that's what he said."

"Who said?" Freya stood as well, trailing the old man through his workshop. "Did my mother talk with you?"

He shook his head and backed away from her. Soren's shoulder clipped one of the shelves, and all the jars that contained shimmering dust rattled where they were kept. "I won't say a word. Not to you, not to anyone."

But that wasn't right! She was here to find her mother, and he knew where she was! Or he'd spoken with her. Something had obviously come to pass. Some reason why he didn't feel like he could tell Freya about her own mother.

It wasn't fair.

It wasn't right.

She hadn't come all this way to be so disappointed because an old man wouldn't tell her what he knew!

Anger blasted out of her in a shattering echo that thundered through the workshop. Energy seared through the air, making the jars rattle even more and blowing Arabella's hair behind her. Even the severed head opened her eyes even wider, as though she was shocked that a mortal had powerful magic.

Freya pressed her shaking hands against her belly and tried to look like she was strong. But really, she was horrified at what she'd done.

Nothing like that had ever happened. Nothing had ever proven so forcefully that both Eldridge and Soren were right. She had magic, and she had no idea how to control it.

"That," Soren said, lifting a gnarled finger and pointing at her. "That is why your mother didn't want you to know where she was."

But that was cruel. And wrong. If her mother knew something about Freya's past that would explain all this, then Freya had a right to know. She had the right to understand why her mother had hidden so much from her daughters.

Her hands were shaking even more now. That anger and disappointment bubbling in her chest.

Soren twisted his hand in the air, and she felt something come down over her shoulders. As though he'd drawn a wet blanket over her that was heavy and lined with... something. Something that wouldn't let her even attempt to use magic.

"No more in my shop," he growled. "I don't care that no one taught you how to control it, little girl. There are too many priceless objects in here for you to break them with carelessness."

Eldridge stood and joined them by the shelves. He put his arm over her shoulders and drew her back to the table. "Sit, Freya. I imagine you are tired after such a show."

She wasn't, that was the strange thing. She'd also thought to be tired by what had happened, but she felt more awake and invigorated than before.

Soren reluctantly met the Goblin King's gaze. "I won't help anymore, if that's what your plan is. I think I've made it very clear where I stand. Sending your untamed witch on me won't change my mind."

"I wouldn't dream of it," Eldridge replied. He held his hands tucked behind his back, ever the gentleman and the politician. "I've been around longer than her, you know that. I'm here to make a trade for information. Not about her mother, but about the wolf. We still need to find it."

Soren narrowed his eyes. "What's the trick, fae?"

"No trick. I want to get out of this damned mining town sooner rather than later. And if that means a trade, then that's what we'll do."

A calculating light bloomed behind the Magician's eyes. "What are you willing to give?"

Freya was the one who answered. "Anything."

Sure, Eldridge could glare at her all he wanted after that declaration, but she meant it. If he asked for her soul in trade for finding out where her mother was, then she would willingly give it.

Perhaps that was her greatest flaw. She would do anything for her family. Even give herself up.

Eldridge sighed and pinched his nose. "We will not give you anything. Ignore my companion's ridiculous statement. But I will let you take a bit of her magic to research it, or add to your own collection. That's up to you, Magician."

Soren vibrated with glee. He burst into movement that was surprisingly swift for a man his age. He charged through the room, grabbing bottles off shelves and holding them in his arms. Though he did pause for a second to whisper something in Arabella's ear. The head closed her mouth and then smiled with a wicked grin.

If that wasn't unsettling, then Freya didn't know what was.

She shivered with disgust as the Magician approached her, a vial outstretched.

"You will not fight me on this," he warned. "It'll only hurt even worse."

She supposed she didn't have a choice.

Freya braced her hands on the arms of the chair and stared straight ahead. The sensation was very similar to when Eldridge had taken power from her back in the Winter Court. It felt like someone was pulling at her soul, yanking off a piece that might have been important, but she wasn't all that certain why.

Her stomach flexed, and Freya felt something coming out of her mouth. Gagging, she opened her lips and a pale mist erupted from her throat. It spiraled through the air toward the small vial the Magician held out.

"Yes," he muttered. "That's it."

Finally, the Magician corked the vial and everything stopped. Freya slammed her back against the chair and heaved in a breath. How strange. How awful.

Soren lifted the vial and watched the mist swirling inside it. "This is impressive. I wonder what I'll find when I really look through it. What do you think it is, Freya?"

Brows furrowed in confusion and fear, she shook her head. "I don't know."

"We'll find out, eventually." He pocketed the mist and then held out a small, circular jar.

There was a tiny light inside it. Freya took the bottle and realized the light was the smallest person she'd ever seen. A tiny woman with glowing skin and bright wings that she gently beat inside the bottle.

Soren tapped the side, and the woman fell onto the bottom of the glass. "A will-o'-the-wisp. Dangerous creatures if not contained, but she'll be able to lead you to the werewolf."

"How?" Eldridge scoffed. "She's a faerie who's likely been in that bottle for many years. You can't expect us to believe she will lead us through the mines."

"She used to work in them. This was one of the faeries who guided miners to their doom. She liked to watch the werewolf tear their wings off." Soren bared his teeth in a dark grin. "When a dwarf captured her in a jar, I paid a pretty price to have her on my shelf. If anyone knows where to go, it's this one."

Freya's stomach churned. Having someone guide them who wanted to see people get killed, felt a little like asking a butcher to watch her pig for a few hours. "How do we know she won't lead us to the slaughter?"

"You don't." Soren waved a hand, and suddenly her chair careened toward the door. "Now get out of my shop."

CHAPTER 17

It took them a while to get back to the inn, but they still beat Arrow. And though their companion had found them some food, Freya didn't feel like she could keep anything down. Not yet, at least.

Her mother had really been here. Now it wasn't just the Spring Maiden claiming that Astrid was in this court.

Suddenly, this all felt too real. She hadn't realized how it would feel to know that she had been lied to. Or perhaps more accurately, that she'd wasted so much time because she'd been certain no one could survive that long in the wild.

Did this mean her father was alive too? Had they both been waiting for her to find them, help them, save them, only to realize that they were alone?

It turned her stomach for days.

Both Arrow and Eldridge agreed they had to wait a little while to go into the mines. They needed the proper tools, and then they needed a guide who could actually get them through without causing a cave in.

Few miners were likely to help them. Arrow had decided he would be the one to talk with the pixies, namely because neither

Freya nor Eldridge looked trustworthy. At least Arrow fit in here with his grubby, dirt smudged nose and constant scowl.

Freya and Eldridge stood out too much. So, they were both stuck in the inn. Together. When all she wanted was to move, and all he wanted was for her to slow down.

It was frustrating, to say the least.

A week later, she wandered to the inn's bar in the hopes that she might find Claude. At least he had pleasant conversation and a bottle of whiskey to spare. She wasn't sure where he was getting all the alcohol, considering it always appeared that he had very few bottles left, but she never failed to find him underneath the bar where he had drank himself the night before.

Unfortunately, it did not appear that Claude was there today. In fact, she couldn't find him at all.

Freya braced herself on the bar and peered underneath it. Nothing. No pixie man and no scent of alcohol either.

"Strange," she muttered. "I thought he would be here."

If he wasn't here, then where in the world was Claude? She wasn't all that confident the pixie man even stayed in one of the rooms. She thought it more likely that he was always close to the bar and the front door.

Whether that was because of his fear for the werewolf, or his fear that someone might steal his alcohol, she'd never know.

Freya straightened and blinked her eyes in shock. The room had changed into something else entirely. Or... well. Somewhere else.

Candles decorated every surface. Wax had splashed around their bases, dripping off the tables and leaking onto the floor in delicate puddles of cream. The warm light danced in a slight breeze that she didn't quite remember feeling before. Tiny faerie lights hung in loose arches from the ceiling like a network of tiny stars.

"What is this?" she murmured, walking around the corner of the bar and out into the main area of the inn.

By the door, a trail of rose petals littered the floor. They led back to the stairs she had walked down just moments ago. More pale candles melted onto the railing of the stairs, delicately creating a lace-like pattern of wax. The rose petals spilled over the stairs as well, leading all the way up the warm wood.

She followed the path to the top of the stairs. A faint tickle trailed from her toes all the way up to her head. Freya lifted her arms and marveled as the Goblin King's magic rewove the fabric of her pants and shirt. He turned the entirety of her clothing into a graceful, silken night dress. Simple but elegant.

What was he up to?

Heat bloomed in her chest. He'd gone through a lot of trouble to make this moment special, and she could only guess at what he wanted.

Freya put her palm on the door and pushed it open. The Goblin King stood in the center of their room, wearing his own matching set of pale silk sleep pants and an unbuttoned shirt. The floor was covered in red rose petals and a fire danced in the hearth, turning the dismal sadness of their room into a warm and inviting place. He held a bouquet of white roses in his hand that he held out for her to take.

"I thought you might want an evening to ourselves," he said, watching his fingers on the thorns. "A lot has happened since we came here, my hero. And for all that we've done, I know you have been overwhelmed."

She took the offered roses and buried her nose in their petals. They smelled like spring, when metal and soot had filled her nose for weeks now. Sighing, she held the roses against her heart. "I suppose it has been a little overwhelming."

"A little?" He raised his brow. "I went through all this work for nothing, then?"

Freya snorted. "You used magic to do all this and we both know it."

"Maybe." Eldridge held out his arm for her to take and guided her toward the fireplace. "But I asked both Arrow and Claude to give us some private time together. They're both out at another establishment, probably getting into horrible trouble if I know my companion."

He was probably right. Arrow loved to enjoy himself when he was given leave.

Setting her fingers on his arm, Freya followed him to the blast of heat that rolled off the fireplace. Together, they sat down on the rose petals that filled the air with their lovely scent. She set the bouquet beside them and sank her fingers into a sheepskin that he'd placed beneath the petals. "You put a lot of effort into this, I'll admit that."

"Thank you." He hesitated, swallowed hard, then asked, "Do you like it?"

For such a powerful man, he could be rather bashful about this. Freya wondered how many times he'd gone out of his way to make a day special for another person. Or even to woo another faerie woman that might have haunted his dreams once.

The flare of jealousy in her chest was a warning to stay away from such thoughts. This was about him and her, not whatever image of perfection her mind conjured up.

Impulsively, she reached out and cupped his face with her hand. "It's perfect, Eldridge. Thank you for thinking about me."

He grinned and tilted his head into her palm. "This isn't all, you know. I wouldn't be so careless as to set this all up without something for us to eat and drink."

With a flourish of his hand, a plate appeared in front of them. It was laden with cheese, meat, and grapes. Another flick of his wrist brought about a glass pitcher full of red wine, and two gold goblets.

"Impressive," she said with a quirk of her brow. "Where did you get all this from?"

"My own court," he replied defensively. "I'm not stealing from anyone, if that's what you're insinuating."

"Just checking." Freya reached for a grape and popped it into her mouth. Flavor exploded on her tongue, far more than she remembered with fruit from the mortal realm. "Is this going to doom me to the faerie realm for good? My mother used to say a person couldn't eat faerie food unless they wanted to be trapped forever."

He reached past her and took a few grapes of his own, setting them on his tongue one by one. "If you're stuck here, then I suppose I am too. I don't think that rumor is true, though. I've seen mortals eat our food and return to their home when their faerie captor grew bored with them."

"Have you? How many mortals have you seen in the faerie realms?" Freya was morbidly curious if there were more people like her. People who had come hoping to save someone, and who had eventually failed.

"Hundreds." Eldridge grinned. "Would you like to hear the stories?"

"Absolutely."

And so they passed the evening with him telling her countless tales about the humans who had tried to win their siblings back. She listened with rapt attention, laughing at the right points and solemnly nodding at their failures.

In a way, all the stories were the same. They either wished away their sibling, or the foolish child had made the same mistake as Esther. Their sibling had traveled all the way to the faerie realm and been given a few tasks by the Goblin King. Some were very difficult, most were rather simple in nature.

No one had bested him until her.

"It's rather sad, don't you think?" She had laid her head in his lap over an hour ago. "They are willing to go through so much trouble to get their family member back, but you always knew they would fail."

"I suppose." Eldridge ran his nails through her hair, gently raking her scalp. "But now I wonder if they were all practice for the moment I would meet you."

What a fanciful thing for him to say. Freya didn't think he was preparing for her. He hadn't even known she was alive! And yet, the questioning expression on his face made her wonder if he was really considering such an insane thought.

"Eldridge," she said, sitting up to look him in the eye. "You don't really think you were preparing for me this whole time, do you? That's a ridiculous thing to say. I wasn't even born when many of these people were in the faerie realm."

"No, you weren't." He cupped her face in his hand, stroking his thumb over the peak of her cheekbone. "But that's how it goes with faeries, you know. We only find someone who completes our souls once in a lifetime. Every step of our existence is preparing us for meeting that person. If we lose them, then it is a fate worse than death. A parting of a soul that has torn into a thousand pieces, never to be healed again."

Her tongue stuck to the roof of her mouth. Was he saying she was his soulmate? Wasn't that as good a declaration of love as she would ever get?

Maybe it was the wine talking, or maybe it was that she'd wanted this for so long, but Freya was finished with talking. He'd made certain that her evening was special and that no matter what, she felt like they were together. Even while hunting a serial killer and tracking down her long lost mother.

She cupped his neck ever so gently. Freya scraped her nails down the back of his head and neck, lingering on the cords of muscles that worked in a swallow. No more words were necessary between them. Not tonight, at least.

Tugging him toward her, she kissed him as if she were trying to brand a promise against his lips. That she would always appreciate his attempts at romance. And no matter how far life drew them away from each other, she would always let her heart sing for him.

He slid his tongue along the seam of her mouth, reaching forward to hold on to her jaw. Freya let him. She flexed her fingers on the back of his neck, then climbed into his lap. One leg on either side of his hips, she finally felt like she was where she belonged.

Eldridge wrapped his arm around her waist, holding her jaw with the other, and slowly rocked himself against her.

Though he was stiff and hard, Freya didn't find herself frightened of what would come next. She'd never been with a man before, had only heard rumors from other girls in the village when they spoke of their secret lovers. She had thought this moment would terrify her.

Instead, all she could think about was the flavor of sugar on his tongue. His hands gripped her waist, not bruising or punishing. Eldridge learned the shape of her body with every gentle press of his fingers.

Wrenching away from her lips, Eldridge pressed his face into the crook of her neck. He inhaled deeply, then set his teeth to the place where her neck met shoulder.

Freya gasped as something happened in her body. A clenching sensation along with a flood that forced her hips to glide against his. Rocking back and forth as she had never done before.

He breathed out a long sigh in her ear. "You are mine, Freya of Woolwich. Mine and mine alone."

"Not yet," she replied. Freya teased the seashell of his ear with her tongue, biting down on the lobe hard before adding, "Not until you make me yours, at least."

His hands flexed on her back and a low growl reverberated through his being. "Don't challenge me, Freya."

Oh, it wasn't a challenge, it was much more than that. Freya wanted him to devour her mind, body, and soul. She wanted to forget that they were in a freezing cold inn and that she didn't know where her mother was. She wanted to forget everything but them for a night.

Licking her lips, she leaned back even as she continued rocking on his lap. "I want to make a deal with you, Goblin King."

His eyes flashed bright silver. "I thought you were done with deals?"

"I guess I'm not after all." Her next words would take more bravery than she felt, but magic pulsed through her veins. Freya swallowed and said, "Make me enjoy this, Goblin King. And I will give you the entire night."

The tufts of hair on his ears moved as though the pointed tips twitched on their own. "Oh, I'll need much more than a single night, Freya."

And with that, the time for talking ended. The fire flared bright behind her back as the Goblin King slid his hands up her thighs. He drew the fabric sensually over her skin. Taking his time so he knew she was feeling every slide of silk. Freya tilted her head back and closed her eyes.

His hands slid higher, drawing the nightgown to her hips and revealing her glistening center to his gaze. She gasped. Eldridge slid a single finger through her folds as his other hand continued to push the silk higher.

Lips and teeth took hold of her nipple as he stroked her core. Freya heard a moan follow a long sigh. She was tense in his arms, waiting for something. Anything. Some peak or tension that she hadn't realized a man could bring her to.

The swirl of magic pressed against her back. She relaxed into the sensation of another set of hands, knowing without a doubt that it was the Goblin King. He drew the nightgown up over her head and then pressed both his palms to her inner thighs, spreading her even farther.

Hours might have passed where he teased her with lips, tongue, and fingers. Or it might have been seconds. She didn't know. All she could focus on was the sensation rising in her body, waiting and hoping that he would listen to her every gasp.

Eldridge rolled her on top of him, then eased his hands down her arms and drew her hands to his shoulders where he pressed them firmly. He stroked his hands down her sides, settling over her hips where he gently lifted her.

She felt the tip of him press against her entrance, but again, no fear. This was what she wanted. No, what she needed.

He didn't move her again. Instead, she felt his hands relax on her hips even as his shoulders shook beneath her hands. He wasn't going to force anything, instead, he was letting her take the lead.

Freya opened her eyes and stared down into that moonlit gaze. She shifted her fingers, tensed her thighs around his hips, and lowered herself onto him. Inch by mind numbing inch.

He shuddered, eyes rolling back in his head. The deep, guttural moan that erupted from his chest sent a zing of electricity to her very core.

When she was fully seated upon him, it felt natural to keep moving. She rose and fell, riding the waves of sensations until she just barely reached a peak. Only to have it fall out of reach. Over and over again.

Finally, he groaned again and took hold of her hip firmly. He held onto her, settling her into a different rhythm, their movements more powerful. Eldridge kept one hand on her hip and eased the other between them, pressing between her legs on some part of her body that made her back arch.

There it was. That was what she had been looking for.

Sweat glistened on both of their skin, and in that moment of rising she thought they both looked like they were covered in diamond dust.

His magic pressed her down harder. His fingers turned bruising as he gripped her, making her move faster while he stroked that impossible place she hadn't realized existed.

She rose higher.

Higher.

Then the stars opened up, and she saw oblivion.

Freya cried out in his grip, holding onto him as he arched into her, plunging deeper a few more times before stilling with his lips pressed against her neck.

It was done, and yet it still felt as though she had been filled with some kind of impossible magic. He was still inside her, stretching her almost to discomfort, and yet... she didn't want to let him go. She didn't want to move from his chest while he held her limp body against his own.

Freya could hear his heart beating against her ear. She tasted the salt of his skin, no longer sweet, but mortal and fae mixed into one.

And she didn't regret what they had done.

Pressing a kiss to his shoulder, she tucked her head into the crook of his neck. "I think you won our deal, Goblin King."

He chuckled, still breathing hard. "Well, at least I beat you once."

Freya didn't even try to stop the smile on her lips. He made her happy, and she couldn't remember the last time she'd felt like this. Or if she had ever been this happy before him.

The Goblin King made her feel real. Like she was more than just a mortal. More than a woman who lived in the forest. She was Freya to him, and he worshipped the very ground she walked on. He'd proven that with every kiss he pressed into her skin.

Eldridge shifted, pulling himself from her and leaving her empty. With a soft moan, she tried not to let him go.

He chuckled, "My dear, I'm just moving us to the bed rather than the floor."

"Why would we do that? The bed is covered with bugs."

He stood, then scooped her up into his arms. "It is not, because I cleaned it. And I believe the deal said I get you all night, now." He grinned down into her shocked expression. "A deal is a deal, Freya."

CHAPTER 18

Freya woke the next morning and reality hit her over the head like a tree had fallen on top of her. She'd slept with the Goblin King. And not just slept, really. They had spent the entire night exploring each other's bodies, learning the sighs and moans that came from each other's lips, and...

Oh god.

She would never get the image of him out of her head. Freya would look at him and every time would remember the tension in his features as he leaned over her. She'd see the cords of his neck as he threw his head back while he was deep inside of her.

Sure, she'd known this was where they were going. Of course they were approaching that singular moment when they would finally taste the forbidden.

Freya just hadn't realized how embarrassed it would make her feel. After all, she was still draped over the Goblin King's chest, completely naked, and he was fast asleep. Likely Eldridge wouldn't feel awkward at all, but how many times had he done this?

She had never felt another person's touch like that. Never been that close to a living being, and... well. It was a little overwhelming. Like everything else in her life.

Freya peeled herself off him, taking care not to wake the sleeping Goblin King. Tip toeing across the room, she gathered her clothing and pulled them on. The nightgown had turned back into her shirt and pants. The flowers and candles had disappeared. The room had returned to the dismal, disappointing atmosphere it had been when they first arrived.

This was where her first time had been. In a mining town's inn. On a bug ridden bed in the middle of nowhere.

Her first time was supposed to be something to remember. Something honorable and wonderful and... and...

Freya shook the thoughts out of her head. Those were romantic things to think about, but real life wasn't a fairytale, nor a romance. If she had wanted to be wooed like that, then she should have approached him when they were both in the Goblin Kingdom. Then she would have had the experience to tell others about.

Shaking her head, she gently opened the door inch by painstaking inch, waiting for the squeaking hinges to wake him. When he remained asleep, she squeezed herself through the small gap and padded down the stairs.

Hopefully Arrow had returned and found something. Then she could get her mind off what they had done. She could focus on the future and put all her mind power into planning their next steps.

As luck would have it, Arrow was waiting for her by the bar. He and Claude were bent over, whispering to each other as if someone might overhear their plotting.

Freya snuck up behind them, then cleared her throat. "What are you two up to?"

Claude straightened so quickly she heard his back crack. He let out a startled squeal, then relaxed when he saw who was standing in front of them. "Miss Freya! You are impressively quiet for a human. I didn't even hear you come downstairs."

The goblin dog sniffed and wagged his tail. "Neither did I,

which is impressive on its own. And we weren't up to anything, I'll have you know."

"I found you two huddled together in the shadows, whispering." Freya lifted a brow. "I'd think that the body language of two faeries up to something."

His eyes canted to the side, and Arrow finally heaved a sigh. "Fine. We were just talking about who was going to wake you two. We need to get going."

She kept her brow lifted and stared him down. That wasn't everything. She wasn't a fool. And he would have to tell her the rest if he wanted her to move. Now, all she had to do was see which one of the faerie men broke first.

Arrow was far too stubborn to give in to her disapproval. He stared right back at her with his own brows furrowed in a glare, teeth slightly bared in an impressive snarl.

But Claude caved like a stack of cards. "We were musing about what we'd find when we interrupted you and the Goblin King. That's all. Arrow thought you two were caught in a lovers' embrace. I thought it more likely you were both exhausted after dealing with the Magician. He's quite terrifying, as you know."

She did know how terrifying the Magician was. Freya wouldn't forget that experience soon, but she was also disappointed that the two faeries were gossiping. How terribly beneath them to speak of her own private life. And time.

Squaring her shoulders, she used her best motherly disappointed face and glared at them. "The Goblin King and my private time is none of your business. Either of you. I think there are more useful things for the both of you to be doing than gossiping about what was happening upstairs."

Eldridge's voice echoed down from the stairs. "Oh, go easy on them, Queen Killer. Curiosity is the natural state of a faerie."

She tensed at the sound of his footsteps approaching them. What was she supposed to say after doing that with him all night? Good job? Should she pat him on the back and congratulate him for spending the entire evening on her body, just as he had said he would?

Awkwardness spread through her until she didn't know what to do with her hands. She crossed them over her chest, then thought that might seem like she was pushing her breasts up for him to look at. So she shifted onto one foot, then felt like he might consider that a rather tantalizing pose.

Arrow watched her every movement, frowned, then looked between the two of them as Eldridge finally joined them. "Good heavens and faerie realms, I was right, wasn't I?"

"Right about what?" she snarled.

"You two—" He waved a paw between them and then pressed it against his mouth. Arrow gagged a little, then added, "You were together."

Panic raced through her veins. She looked at Eldridge, then back at the goblin dog. "Stop it, Arrow."

Eldridge tossed an arm over her shoulders and tugged her against his side. "What's the matter? I don't care if he knows. Let them talk. We're the only two that know what actually happened last night."

If he continued talking, she was going to burst into flames. Her cheeks already burned so hot she was afraid they would sear. "All of you stop it. I don't want to talk about this in front of an audience."

The grin on Eldridge's face was far too proud. She hadn't even said he had done a good job, yet he was acting like she had called him a god. This wasn't fair. She didn't want to publicize her private life!

She shook his arm off her and stepped away from them all. "I'll say it one last time, I'm not talking about this with all of you."

Every face in the room fell. As if they all suddenly realized that she was very uncomfortable and they were the ones who had made her feel that way. Good, let them be guilty. They'd all stepped out of line and she wanted them to feel bad about it.

Crossing her arms over her chest, Freya hugged herself tight. "Arrow, did you find someone who can bring us to the mines?"

He was staring at her with those sorrowful eyes. Obviously he knew he'd done something wrong, but he didn't know what that wrong thing was. Finally, he cleared his throat and nodded. "Yes, I think I did. I still think it'll be equally dangerous, but at the very least, we won't get lost."

Good, at least she could focus on that rather than the knowledge that everyone now knew she lost her virginity. Idiots.

Freya knew they had meant nothing by it. They were all merely happy that their loved ones had taken a step toward being more of a couple and less of two people trying to figure out where the other person was. She understood that. But publicly talking about it all?

She had to draw the line somewhere.

Wincing, she took a step back and leaned against the bar. "Who is it?"

He shook his head, ears flopping against the side of his cheeks before replying. "Well, there aren't a lot of savory sorts around here, so I will say I'm not sure that we can entirely trust him. But he works in the mines, and said he goes to the areas most won't because that's where the good mirror ore is."

Eldridge turned his gaze from her and frowned at the goblin dog. "Why does he go where others won't? That seems suspicious."

"I thought the same," Arrow replied. "But he wants to get out of here, so he's willing to take risks others won't. He said he needs to get back to his family sooner rather than never. The more ore he gathers, the better it is. He'd rather get the money and run, even if it costs the tunnel collapsing on his head."

Freya wasn't entirely opposed to following a risk taker like that. It sounded as though the pixie knew how to get around the mines, and that's what they needed. The tunnels were where the werewolf hid. And potentially where her own mother waited for them to save her.

"All right," she said, bracing her fists on her hips. "So he thinks he can take us through the mines, and perhaps to the werewolf?"

"Maybe." Arrow looked up at Claude, then back to them. "I've yet to find a pixie who will really talk about the beast. They're all terrified of him."

Claude snorted and headed to the back of the bar where he kept his spirits. "And for good reason. A lot of the older pixies refuse to talk about the beast because they're certain even mentioning his name will summon him to your house. I'd keep your voice down if you're saying the word in the mines. They're more likely to kill you for speaking the wolf's name than guide you through the tunnels."

"So we need to keep it quiet that we're hunting the beast." Freya tapped a finger to her chin, still angling her body away from the others. "How are we going to convince this pixie to take us where we need to go, then?"

Arrow coughed into his paw, then sat down on all fours. "That's the problem, unfortunately. We're not going to convince any miners to take us where the werewolf is hiding. For two reasons. The first being that none of them know where he is. The second is that... well. This was the only miner I could find who would guide us at all, and he'll only take us to where they build the mirrors. Anything else, any other exploring, he made it very clear that we're on our own."

Right. Of course. Because why would it be so easy as to have a guide that would take them directly to the creature they were hunting.

She lifted her hands and cracked her knuckles. "Then how in the world are we going to find the wolf?"

"Easy." Eldridge reached into his pocket and drew out the tiny faerie trapped in the jar. She was bright blue today with her hands pressed on the glass walls that kept her away from the fresh air. "I do believe that's why the Magician gave her to us, after all. She's going to lead us directly to the werewolf. Aren't you, my dear?"

The will-o'-the-wisp stuck out her tongue at the Goblin King, then sat down hard on her bottom. She ignored all of them staring at her, and Freya worried that meant she wasn't planning on helping at all.

That little faerie creature was their last hope of finding the werewolf before the monster found them.

Sighing, she turned her gaze up to the ceiling and sent a silent prayer to the heavens. "I guess there's no time like the present, then. Shall we go find our pixie guide?"

CHAPTER 19

They left Claude at the inn with a hefty purse full of gold and a few hugs goodbye. He'd teared up a little when they left, saying how he wished they would find Freya's mother and thanking them for giving him the chance to leave this horrible place.

Freya could only hope it was enough money to get him home. Of all the people she'd met here thus far, Claude had made a special impact on her. The kindly alcoholic deserved a little happiness in his life. At whatever cost.

Arrow led them through the winding streets, past multiple stores and a hundred faeries with haunted eyes. The deeper they got into Mudgate, the worse poverty she saw.

If only they could help all of them. More than taking care of the murderous werewolf plaguing their home.

Finally, Arrow paused in front of a door that was cut crooked so it fit into the wall that was nearly falling over. "He lives here. Said to meet him early if we wanted to have a guide." Arrow's nose twitched. "He didn't say what early was, though. Hopefully, we're not too late."

The door slammed open at the end of his words. "You are

late, dog. But I had a feeling you were coming and free gold is free gold."

The pixie who stepped out to lock the door was entirely unexpected. Freya was used to their kind looking delicate and beautiful. Like the petal of a flower plucked from the stem.

She couldn't guess what flower this man had come from, but maybe it was something thorny.

He was huge. His shoulders spanned the entire doorway and then some, so large that he'd had to tilt his body to get out of his house. And rather than the zipper she was used to seeing the pixies wearing ragged silver scars were visible through his threadbare shirt. His dark skin glistened around the marks, as though magic was trying to heal him and to grow back the wings that had once been there.

Had he ripped them off himself? Or had someone else surgically taken them off?

Freya tried to wipe the disgust from her face, but she feared she wasn't very successful. She couldn't understand how someone willingly gave up a part of themselves that was so beautiful. So rare.

He turned around and yellow eyes stared her down. "Well? You said you wanted to go into the mines, didn't you?"

Why was he looking at her?

Freya looked to her companions, then back to the pixie. "I do want to search the mines. My mother is said to still be in there, and I plan on finding her."

The pixie never looked away from her gaze. Those piercing yellow eyes saw through her words and into the quaking of her very soul. "If your mother was lost in the mines, you aren't going to find her."

"I think I will." She straightened her shoulders and refused to let him intimidate her. She would find her mother if that was the very last thing she ever did. Just because he was a miner, didn't mean he knew everything about the place.

Apparently, he thought differently. The miner snorted, then

shrugged. "Sure. If you want to get lost in the mines with her, be my guest. Follow me to the mirrors and that's where we part ways. I'm not looking for a woman foolish enough to get her head turned around by the mirror ore."

And with that, he walked away from them. He didn't even look over his shoulder to see if they were following him.

Freya looked at Eldridge, who shrugged. He started after the miner with a quick statement tossed over his shoulder. "I guess we better follow him."

She supposed that was one way to look at it, but if this man was so certain they were paying him for nothing, shouldn't he actually play the part of a guide? At least he could tell them something about the mines.

Hurrying to catch up with the man, she strode beside him and reached out a hand for him to shake. "My name is Freya. What shall we call you?"

"Whatever you want to call me, human." He didn't even look at her. "We won't know each other for long enough to care what the other's name is."

"Why would you think that?" she asked, frowning. He could at least pretend that he was interested in their plight.

Surely it wasn't often that a human and two goblins ended up in the Spring Court asking someone to take them into the mines. He must have been at least a little curious about... well. Anything.

The miner shook his head. "I'm going to make it out of the mines tonight with more coins than usual. I'll eat my dinner, then rest my head on my pillow and forget I ever met you."

Disgruntled by how rude this man was, Freya clenched her teeth and snarled, "And you think I will remember you?"

"No." The miner turned down a side street sharply. "I don't think you'll leave the mine at all. You'll be in that cold, barren place, wondering if you should have listened to me in the first place. People like you don't belong in the mines, human. You'll be lucky to see the sun again."

Eyes wide, she tripped over her own feet. The miner stomped away and turned another sharp corner. Disappearing for a few moments before she could catch up with him again.

Eldridge put his hand on her shoulder and forced her to step back. "I don't think he wants to talk with you, my dear."

She couldn't imagine why. She was an unusual creature in this world, and he was about to bring them into a mine where he thought they would die. The least he could do was give them decent conversation. This man was so rude that it made her blood boil.

Frowning, she followed the miner quietly and tried not to take this personally. After all, they had a long way to go, and the miner seemed like he knew where he was taking them. At the very least, they would get to their destination in one piece.

The streets opened up to a wide area that looked as though a giant had taken a huge chunk out of the earth. She stared, wide eyed, watching as pixies zipped out of the cavernous maw with silver chunks of metal in their hands. The one nearest to her brought his large piece to a giant melting pot to their right. He dropped it in, made eye contact with another pixie who nodded, and then he flew back into the cavernous maw of the earth. Apparently to search for more.

The sun overhead wasn't quite as bright as it should be, though. The steam that came off the melting pot filled the air with a cloudy, thick substance.

Their miner grunted. "Don't breathe it in."

"Breathe what in?" Freya asked.

He pointed to the clouds. "That. Mirror magic is dangerous for faeries to inhale. I haven't got the faintest idea what it would do to you if you breathed it in."

Tip understood. She wouldn't take the risk.

Freya trailed along behind him, watching the miners with wide eyes. She was stunned that they could move so quickly. Some of the miners weren't using their wings. Most, actually.

Even their miner got into a cart system that brought the others into the darkness of the earth.

The system was strange. She'd seen tracks like this before, but they were always for wealthy people to move around the kingdom. These rungs were rickety at best, and the cart was held together by steel bars. At least that looked sturdy enough. The seats were plain boards, uncomfortable and designed to be useful rather than aesthetically pleasing.

He gestured for them to sit in it with him. "Come on, then, There's no other way into the mines for the likes of us."

Freya waited for her companions to get in before settling against Eldridge's side. Her curiosity burned too hot to not ask, "Why don't you use your wings like some of the other faeries? It seems like it would be faster for you to gather ore and bring it back."

The miner glared at her, then reached forward for the center pull. "I don't owe you any answers, human. Remember that."

With a quick tug, the cart careened on the tracks down into the shadows.

Wind whistled in her hair and Freya's stomach rose into her throat. She let out a long scream that was stolen by the air blasting past them. She could see nothing but darkness. Shadows that moved in the distance, perhaps that were miners or... she didn't know. All she could think about was the speed that they were rolling on these tracks and how difficult it would be to stop this ridiculous cart from hitting the bottom.

Lights appeared on all sides. She caught glimpses of miners with their pickaxes, hacking away at the earth in the hopes that they would find some magical ore that would give them the ability to get back to their family. Just a nugget. Anything that could be put into that giant melting pot.

The cart slowed, and the lights illuminated their miner, who had leaned forward to grasp the brake system. Freya's stomach dropped back where it belonged, and she could breathe again.

Now that her back wasn't pressed against the cart, she could look around.

One of the pixies lifted his lantern high, illuminated the small piece of ore in his hand. It was silver and beautiful, but steam rose off it like it was hot. Considering he held it with a bare hand, she assumed it wasn't heat that was rolling off the metal. Instead, it had to be magic.

The miner gave another quick tug, and the cart rolled into a large chamber in the center of the mine. Metal squealed as they slowed again, but they stopped smoothly and with no jolt at the end.

"Here we are," he growled, hopping out of the cart and heading over to a large bucket that held a bunch of pickaxes and leather bags. "Good luck finding your mother, human. You'll need it."

She was still angry that he wasn't at least helping them any further. Was he incapable of feeling pity?

Stomping over to his side, she watched as he picked up an axe and held it up to the light. His skin gleamed like he was made of ore as well. Perhaps the mirror magic had rubbed off on this pixie who took his time inspecting his weapon of choice.

"Well?" she asked, fists on her hips. "Don't you have any words of advice for us as we wander through this labyrinth?"

"Not really." He dropped the axe down onto his shoulder and met her gaze. "Don't wander off like your mother. They aren't forgiving, and no one is going to save you. If you scream, no one will hear you. No one but the wolf, that is. And if you want to find him, well, then you're just asking to be killed. Aren't you, little sparrow?"

With a jaunty whistle, he headed off for an empty mine shaft and left her standing there with her mouth open.

Eldridge joined her, chuckling though he was at least trying not to be too loud. "Miners aren't exactly the pixies you're used to, are they?"

She tried to close her mouth, but couldn't quite get over how rude that miner had been. "I don't understand. Why does everyone around here think that I'm going to get killed?"

He wrapped his arm around her shoulder and tucked her into his side. "Because they don't know the Queen Killer, my hero. No one has heard your story, and they're underestimating you."

Freya let him draw her away from the mines and back toward the center chamber, but something twisted in her stomach. Something that made her feel a twinge of fear for the first time since they'd been hunting this monster.

What if the miner was right?

CHAPTER 20

"I think the smartest way to proceed is to ensure we have some direction to go," Arrow said. He drew them away from the cart system and padded through the tunnels with his nose in the air like he was actually a dog.

The wind had blown his fur up in comical directions. He looked very much like he'd been struck by lightning. Of course, he didn't care what he looked like when they were about to go into the tunnels to hunt a beast, but Freya still thought it was funny.

"Where are we going?" she asked.

"The miners said this tunnel would lead us to where the mirrors are created. If anyone knows the older tunnels, it's the dwarves." Arrow's ears perked up, standing straight on his head as he listened for any sound ahead of them. "The wonderful thing is that I adore dwarves. I'm very much looking forward to seeing some again."

Eldridge grabbed onto her arm and forced her to slow down. They lingered in the tunnel far away from Arrow, but still let him lead.

"What is it?" Freya turned toward those starry eyes and tried to keep them moving forward at a quicker pace. "I'm not talking about last night if that's what you're about to insist."

"No, I don't want to talk about last night," he hissed. "I'm trying to warn you about the dwarves."

"Arrow likes them. How bad could they be?" She remembered the stories her mother used to tell her about the creatures. They were wonderful beings with talents in metal and jewelry. Their only rivals were the goblins themselves.

Everyone knew goblin jewelry was cursed, though. That's why no self-respecting human would buy or take anything goblin made. Wearing such a gift would curse the wearer, and who knows what kind of curse that would end up being?

The dwarves were good, talented creatures who had moved into the faerie realms only because there were so few magical creatures left in the mortal realm. At least, that's what her mother always said.

"Arrow doesn't always have perfect taste," Eldridge hissed. "Dwarves are territorial at best. Just... keep quiet when we meet them, would you? They don't like humans, and Arrow has clearly forgotten that."

She thought he was overreacting. The Goblin King worried about her more than she worried about herself.

Rolling her eyes, Freya hurried to catch up to Arrow. "Sure. I'll be careful, as always."

If she wasn't mistaken, he muttered, "You're never careful," before catching up with her.

The tunnel opened up to the most incredible cavern. Large white marble pillars filled the space and connecting planks created walkways where hundreds of dwarves moved quickly. Hung on giant wires in between these columns was almost a hundred mirrors as well.

They were in every shape and size. Some circular, some large and rectangular. Some of them were even the size of her palm with ornate frames and tin handles.

The dwarves were rather unusual in shape and speed. They

all had beards, even the women with their prominent breasts. Their legs were shorter than human legs, but she was surprised that they were still quite tall. In fact, they would have come up to her shoulder. Most of them, at least.

One of the dwarves raced by them, shouting to get out of the way because he was handling hot metal.

She jumped to the side and narrowly missed the steaming cloud of mirror magic that followed the dwarf.

"How can they breathe that in?" she asked.

Eldridge shrugged and held out his arm for her to go ahead of him. "Dwarves aren't like the rest of us. I hesitate to even call them fae. The rules don't apply to their kind. They can lie, cheat, steal. Their tongues aren't locked by the same magic as my kind and for that, it's hard to trust them."

She tilted her head to the side and raised a brow. "Do you not trust me? I can lie."

"I'm certain you can." He rubbed a hand over the back of his neck. "But I like to think you wouldn't lie to me. If given the chance."

Freya's face split with a blinding smile. "You're right. I wouldn't lie to you."

"Good." Together, they braved one of the strange wooden walkways and followed Arrow as his voice rang through the cavern.

"I love dwarves!" the goblin dog shouted. "Look at these mirrors. Are they not the most magical things you've ever seen?"

Freya couldn't take her eyes off them. Some of the mirrors seemed to have something, or someone, inside them. Shadows moved behind the glass. They twisted like a person was watching them traverse through the cavern.

She didn't know if she should be frightened or not. These weren't just magic mirrors. They were living things.

The dwarves weren't using their magic to create mirrors like in the stories. Mirrors that could tell the future or predict who a princess would marry. These mirrors had a mind of their own, and she could feel their power every time they walked by one.

It was unnerving.

Unnatural.

And yet, she still wanted to wake one up and see what it had to say to her. What if the mirror knew where her mother was?

"Freya." Eldridge put his hand on her shoulder and drew her away from the large standing mirror. "They're very mesmerizing to look at, but their magic is dangerous. You need to keep your wits about you in this place. Do you hear me?"

She did, but it was so hard not to look in the mirror. There was a shadow behind the glass in the shape of a woman. Was the mirror trying to tell her where her mother was? What if the mirror was already reaching out? Trying to get her to see where her mother had been hidden?

This was her moment. She just had to ask the mirror what she wanted and then... and then...

Two hands slapped both sides of her cheeks. Freya lunged away from the painful ache, blinking her eyes and holding her face in her hands. "What?" she snarled.

And there, standing in front of her, was a dwarf.

This must be a female dwarf because her breasts were rather impressive. Her beard was shorter than the others, trimmed neatly to her face and gelled swirls on her cheeks. Her dark hair was nearly black as night, and her searing blue eyes burned with anger. "What do you think you're doing, looking into a mirror like that?"

She had a thick accent with lilting tilts at the ends. Freya might have even enjoyed listening to the woman speak if she hadn't been scolding.

Still rubbing her cheeks, Freya frowned down at the other woman. "What do you mean? It's rather hard not to look into them. Don't you think?"

Eldridge pressed a hand to his mouth, snickering behind the dwarf. Why hadn't he helped Freya? After all they had done last night, she expected him to be a little more protective. He should have jumped to her defense and tossed the dwarf into the darkness below them.

But no. Of course not. The Goblin King was snickering into his hand like a child because Freya had been slapped twice at the same time.

She'd get him back later.

The dwarf planted her hands firmly on her hips and shook her head in disapproval. "This is why mortals aren't allowed in the mines. You get too wrapped up in the magic, and then what are we supposed to do? Make sure you don't wake up an evil mirror? It's not my job."

"Then what is your job?" Freya asked. She finally dropped her hands from her cheeks, even though they still stung horribly.

"I make the mirrors," the dwarf snarled. "And apparently now I'm supposed to watch you and make sure you don't break anything."

Freya had less intent on breaking any magic mirrors than she did dying in these mines. She knew how much bad luck she'd get from breaking a normal mirror, let alone one that had a mind of its own. "I'm not going to break anything."

"Accidents happen, and then you find yourself trapped in a dimension you didn't know existed." The dwarf walked away from them, shaking her head. "Follow me, would you? And stop trying to touch things."

She looked back to Eldridge, who shrugged, then followed the dwarven woman. Apparently they now had a new guide, and they hadn't even had to ask for one.

Speaking of... She frowned and called out, "You wouldn't have seen a black and white dog around, would you? I apparently lost my companion."

"Oh, he's waiting for us." The dwarf shouted back. "He's the one who found me and said you were getting yourself in trouble."

Freya sighed. Of course Arrow had said she'd gotten herself in trouble. He was worse than the Goblin King.

They picked their way across the ramparts and through the columns. Freya made sure she wasn't looking at any of the mirrors this time, lest they capture her attention so thoroughly that she couldn't break free. Besides, she didn't want to get slapped by that dwarf again.

The woman was stronger than she looked.

"Are we going to a tunnel?" she asked, leaning to look around Eldridge to the smaller dwarf ahead of him.

"We're going to the place where we keep all the finished mirrors. The ones we've put to bed." The dwarf rolled her eyes and picked up her pace. "My name is Rose, by the way. I make all the handheld mirrors here. The ones that are particularly dangerous for your kind."

"Ah." Freya smiled. "My name is Freya. This is Eldridge. He's—"

"A goblin friend," the Goblin King interrupted her. "I found her in the woods."

"The woods?" Freya mouthed when he looked back at her.

She could understand that he might not want the dwarves to know who he was. That was fine. The Goblin King in the mirror mines might make a few people feel a little uncomfortable. Especially if they hated having a human here this much.

But the woods?

Rose the dwarf chuckled, and the sound was the happiest she had made thus far. "That sounds like a mortal. She wandered into the Autumn Court then, hm?"

Eldridge laughed with her, likely at the thought of Freya being foolish enough to do that. "Something along those lines. It's a story we'll gladly tell you in return for a few directions."

"Yes, your goblin dog has already told us all of your plight. It's a horrible thing what happened to her mother." Rose's expression fell into one of great sadness. "I think we might be able to help you, but I fear you may already be too late. The werewolf likes to eat quickly, you see. His hunger is impossible to sate."

The words shivered down Freya's spine. She hurried to follow the dwarf into another cavern that opened up before them. This one ended with stairs leading to the floor, where countless mirrors stood with blankets over their reflective surfaces. Effectively hiding them from anyone who might seek to use their magic.

Freya thought it was rather adorable. The dwarves had actually put the mirrors to bed.

Rose stood in front of the largest mirror and planted her hands on her hips. She watched them with an angry expression, then blew out a breath. "Arrow, I believe you are hiding behind a mirror somewhere. You'll have to come out to listen rather than sneaking about like you've been doing."

The soft, padding sound of dog feet could be heard. A small black and white dog looked around a mirror to their right, his expression one of sincere apology. "I know that, Rose. I was just looking around. How often does one get an opportunity to be around this many magic mirrors?"

"Never, unless you're a dwarf. The three of you won't speak a word of this to anyone else either, do you understand?" The glare on the dwarf's face made it hard to think of doing anything other than agreeing with her.

Arrow joined them, and they all nodded their heads forcefully.

"Good," Rose snarled. "Then I will help you. And only because this werewolf is a threat to all magic mirrors. If he continues destroying the pixie population, then we will never get the ore we need. Dwarves are not miners. We are artists. I'm going to make that very clear right now in case any magical law enforcement gets their hands on your memories. I am doing this to help the dwarves and everyone else who might ever want to use a magical mirror."

Apparently whatever Rose planned on helping them with was breaking every dwarven rule in the book. Freya knew she should be solemn in this moment, and thankful that anyone would be willing to take this risk. But really, she was excited. Fueled by the energy in the room.

Rose pointed at Freya. "You. Come here and stand in front of this mirror."

"You said it was dangerous for a human to do that," she replied, trying very hard to not be too snarky.

"How adorable. The human remembers things." Rose rounded the mirror's edge and grabbed onto the sheet. "You'll be with me the entire time. I made this mirror when I was first apprenticing and learning how my magic can give life to metal. He won't dare harm you if I'm here."

It was a small reassurance, but Freya also realized it was the only one she was going to get.

Stepping up to the mirror, she took a deep breath and watched as the sheet fell away. This standing mirror had to be at least eight feet high. It towered over her with a silver ornate frame that was decorated with thousands of lilies. They might have been beautiful if Freya also didn't know how poisonous those flowers were.

This mirror was meant to be beautiful and deadly.

It heaved in a shuddering sigh and then a man stepped into view. He stood behind her reflection, and Freya belatedly realized that her two companions weren't in the mirror. It was only herself and the magic mirror right now.

He wasn't anyone she might have thought to be so powerful. The man had mousy brown hair and a soft, trustworthy smile. He wore a white peasant's shirt and brown pants. His features were unremarkable. If she had seen him in a crowd and someone asked her to point him out again, Freya didn't think she'd be able to. Maybe that was the magic.

"Hello," she said. "My name is Freya."

"And I'm your magic mirror," he replied. "What is it you seek?"

This all felt rather easy. She'd thought it would be difficult to convince the mirror to help her, or Rose. But they were all working together to get her to the werewolf... why? Because he was a plague upon the pixies?

She supposed that would make sense. Freya was so unused to faeries being helpful. But Eldridge had claimed the dwarves weren't fae at all, so maybe that was why this one was kinder.

"I'm looking for my mother," she said. Not the werewolf at all, but they were intertwined. No matter what she did, the werewolf always led back to her mother.

"Ah," the mirror said. "That's not what I was expecting you to say at all. Rose claimed you were looking for the wolf."

"I was." Freya felt like she was talking through water. Her voice wasn't loud enough, no matter how much she shouted. "I am. I want to stop the wolf, but I also want to find my mother."

"It's an interesting question, you see. Your mother's fate and that of the wolf are... the same. In a way." He frowned, shaking his head. "Even my magic cannot break through the guise of enchantment that wraps around your mother. She is hidden, covered in fur and flowers. It seems."

"Flowers?" The fur she could understand. After all, the werewolf had kidnapped her. Of course she would end up in some place that was full of the beast's shed. But flowers?

"Yes. In a meadow of sorts, I suppose that means she's in the Spring Court."

"In a way," Freya corrected. "She's here in the mines."

He frowned, and the background changed. He was suddenly in a tunnel, not like the one she stood in, but dark and dank. Stalactites hung from the ceiling and water dripped down on his shoulder. "This is the place that will bring you to her, but I cannot go any farther."

"This is one of many tunnels," she sighed. "I cannot find her if you don't give me more direction than that."

"My magic is strong. But whatever hides your mother from my gaze is far stronger."

Rose stepped into view behind Freya. "Can you show us more of the tunnel? I might know which one it is."

The mirror man nodded. "I can."

He moved to the side and Freya noticed a few adjoining tunnels split into this one. In a particular tunnel there was a minecart still full of ore, and a large cave in behind it. At the top of the ore pile was a single gemstone, glowing bright blue.

"There we go," Rose murmured. "I know exactly what tunnel this is."

CHAPTER 21

Rose brought them to an ancient tunnel in the cave system. Warning signs hung from every sturdy rock they could.

"Don't go this way."

"Danger ahead."

"Falling rocks and cave-ins."

This was the last place Freya wanted to be. It seemed of all places in the mine, this was the one that was the most danger-ous. The pixies had over mined this area. Shafts overlapped and caused cave-ins. Every step was a cautionary one, and no matter how far ahead she moved, there was always the risk the next step would be her last.

Swallowing hard, she stayed very close to her companions and their guide. "How much farther?" she asked.

"Not much longer until we reach the place the mirror showed us," Rose replied. "But there's a lot farther for you to go after that, I imagine."

Eldridge touched a hand to the pocket where he kept the jarred faerie. "I think we'll be all right. We still have a few tricks up our sleeves to find the wolf."

The look the dwarf gave Eldridge was unimpressed. She

knew he had more tricks, and she wasn't happy about it. "Just don't cause another cave in, you hear me? There are a lot worse things than the werewolf in this mine, and I understand if you have to run. But a cave in here might cause another one farther down. There are still people working nearby. They don't deserve death because all of you couldn't be careful like I warned you."

Maybe this was what the miner had warned them about. They were going into the mines, ones that had certainly caved in already, and that threat was the nightmare of novices like them.

Now, she could only hope that they all stepped carefully.

The darkness threatened to devour their torches. Every shadow shifted and moved on its own. Freya didn't know if that was because hidden ore still remained in the walls of this cave, or if her mind was playing tricks on her.

The walls weren't filled with anything. They were just stone. She had to keep telling herself that.

"Watch your head," Rose called back to them.

Arrow didn't have to, but Freya and Eldridge both put their hands over their heads to touch the ceiling. It got lower and lower until she was walking bent over. That's when Rose stopped guiding them and moved to the other side of the tunnel.

"This is the place," she said.

There was a tunnel that was caved in, but Freya didn't see the cart. "This can't be the place. We're missing the cart filled with ore."

Rose pointed to the collapsed tunnel. "It's behind those rocks."

"Then how are we supposed to get there?"

The dwarf set her pack down and pulled out a few lanterns. "Take these and look in the other tunnels. You want to find the cart, that's the first start. And then you can continue down the tunnel the mirror showed you behind the cart."

"No." Freya shook her head in disbelief. "You were supposed to bring us to the same tunnel. You said you knew where we needed to go."

"I did." Rose finished up placing all the objects on the ground, lit one lantern, and then dusted off her hands. "And I've gotten you as close as I know how. All the other tunnels are too dangerous. If you want to risk your life, then by all means. Do so. I won't go a step further."

She didn't give any of them a chance to argue. The dwarf disappeared back down the tunnel as if the jaws of the werewolf were gnashing at her feet. And then they were alone in the dark, yet again.

Freya couldn't have been more shocked if the dwarf had smacked her cheeks again before leaving. They had a guide for all of a few heartbeats before they were back on their own in the mines.

"You'd think she would have left us with a map at least," Freya snarled.

"There are no maps of this place," Eldridge corrected. "There are no maps of any mines. Those who work here, know the way. And those that don't? They get lost and someone eventually finds their body when they reopen the tunnels."

Well, that was ominous.

Freya stared into the darkness at the networks of shafts that splintered off all over the place. She couldn't guess which one would lead around the cave in and back down the tunnel they needed to walk into.

"Which way should we go?" she asked.

Both Arrow and Eldridge looked at each other, then settled down on the ground beside the lanterns. Why were they sitting? They still had a long journey ahead and stopping now would only be a waste of time. What if her mother needed them and they got there too late?

"Freya," Eldridge coaxed. "We can't go any farther until we get some rest. All of us need sleep."

"I'm not tired." She leaned down and reached for a lantern. "Resting now isn't an option. We have to keep moving."

He put his hand over hers, stopping her from lifting the

metal light. "We will. Once we all rest our minds so we can manage this labyrinth appropriately. If we go into this blind, tired, and full of fear, we will get lost."

Her hand shook in his grip. "What if the werewolf finds us in the middle of this tunnel?"

"And I thought it impossible for you to let fear decide your actions." Eldridge tugged her down onto the stone floor beside him. "Rest your head, Freya. We have to do this or we will make a grave mistake."

She didn't agree. Not at all.

But she also realized there was no argument here. She could try to navigate the tunnels alone, and she would most likely find herself lost within moments. She could take the jarred faerie. Wander through the tunnels following the bright light and hope the will-o'-the-wisp wouldn't lead her to certain death. But what would she do if the tunnel caved in? There would be no one to help her. No one to know.

Freya sat down with them and kept her mouth shut. She didn't argue, even though she disagreed with this choice. She kept her head down and decided it was smarter to listen to the faeries.

Both Eldridge and Arrow fell asleep quickly. She listened to the steady sound of their breathing and reminded herself that they were all safe. This place hadn't bested them yet, even though it had tried many times.

The dwarf had to be a cruel hearted woman to bring them all the way here and then dump them. She'd asked Rose for help! The mirror had seemed like it wanted to assist them as well, but Freya realized that very few people in the Spring Court were interested in helping those they did not know.

She settled on the ground beside her companions and let her mind wander away from this terrifying tunnel with all its threats of death. Her thoughts drifted back to an evening with the Goblin King, where he had only been interested in attending to her every whim and desire.

Freya didn't know how much time passed in that dreaming world. She remembered every detail of their secret night where they had finally explored every inch of each other's body. The sounds of his voice rang in her ears as she rolled over and opened her eyes.

Arrow was curled up in the crook of her body. His head laid on one of her arms and his breathing remained deep and quiet. He was a lovely little animal, even if he wasn't really a dog, her heart still twisted at the sight of his adorable sleeping face.

She rolled a bit more, trying not to disturb the goblin dog while also searching for Eldridge. She wouldn't put it past the blasted man to go off on his own while the two of them were asleep.

He had moved while she dreamed, rolling so his back was facing her. His ribs lifted and fell in the comfort of deep sleep. Thank all the faerie realms that he hadn't done the same thing she would have done. Sneaking away would only cause them all to waste even more time.

As she watched, Freya noted a slight difference in the shadows beyond Eldridge. Had he cast an illusion over them before they fell asleep? It would make sense for them to be protected.

Then the shadows parted and red glowing eyes appeared.

Freya opened her mouth to shout at Eldridge that the werewolf was here. But she couldn't move. She couldn't speak. She couldn't do anything but watch as the beast stepped out of the darkness and loomed over the man she was falling in love with.

The werewolf was just as terrifying as she remembered. His broad chest was covered in hair, his legs bent at an awkward angle, and his wolf head was too large. Too real.

The beast's lips quivered, then parted to reveal shiny teeth that gleamed with drool. A long strand of spittle dripped from his mouth as he leaned over Eldridge. The Goblin King was still asleep.

The man she loved barely reacted as the werewolf leaned

over him. A monster's snarl echoed through the shaft. Freya shivered in fear and realized she still couldn't move. She was frozen in place. Completely at the mercy of this monster who wanted to kill her and everyone she loved.

She couldn't breathe.

Eldridge, she wanted to call out. Wake up!

Those teeth gnashed above Eldridge's face, lingering over his neck as though the monster wanted to tear into the Goblin King. He wanted to cause pain and see blood pool on the floor. Freya could sense that.

But the beast stopped at the last second. He froze, then looked over at her with red, terrifying eyes.

An emotion flickered in the depths of those wild orbs. Freya almost thought the monster recognized her. As if it knew she was the same mortal it had seen in the meadow, the same one whose name he knew.

Deep, guttural tones shook the beast's throat. And yet again, just like last time, the werewolf growled, "Freya."

With a gasp, Freya sat straight up. Arrow tumbled off her lap with a grumble of complaint before he rolled back over onto his side. She sucked in air and wildly turned to look at Eldridge. But he wasn't asleep on his back. He was facing her on his side with his arm outstretched, as if even in his sleep he was trying to hold her hand. There was no beast leaning over him. No werewolf in the darkness.

She'd been dreaming.

Slapping a hand to her forehead, Freya eased back down onto the ground. She'd had a nightmare, and of course she would in this place. Her mind was in turmoil, even in sleep. All she needed to do was calm down a bit.

Her heart continued to race in her chest. She was terrified that Eldridge had almost died, even though she knew very well that wasn't how it worked. Dreams weren't premonitions. Dreams were her mind sorting through all the things she'd thought or learned the day before. Easy as that.

Blowing out a long breath, she rolled Arrow over until he was closer to their heads. Then she gently crawled over Eldridge so she was the big spoon. She put her own back to the darkness because she didn't think the werewolf would hurt her.

The thought was crazy. The werewolf was a monster, and he would hunt down anything that stood before him. Everyone they'd met had said so.

But the recognition in his eyes, at least the first time she'd seen him, made her hesitate. It was more than knowing her. Those eyes were familiar, kind, and full of love. She'd seen them before, she just couldn't remember where.

Shaking her head, she turned so her back was pressed against Eldridge's and met the darkness head on. She stared into the darkness, unafraid. Let them try to intimidate her. Freya had seen more terrifying things than her own nightmares, and she was not the same weak little girl who flinched from shadows.

This time the shadows remained still and quiet. No red eyes stared back at her, and she knew for certain this time that the werewolf had not visited them.

"It was just a dream," she whispered. "Nothing more than that, Freya. Go back to sleep."

She closed her eyes and nudged a little closer to Eldridge. Like him, she stretched out her arm and laid her head on her bicep as a pillow.

Just as she was drifting off to sleep, she realized her hand rested upon a small tuft of coarse fur.

CHAPTER 22

They all woke at almost the same time. As if someone had rung a bell through the tunnel, all three of them sat straight up, gasping for air and reaching for each other.

Freya didn't ask what the other two had dreamt. She knew. Of course, she knew. They'd all had the same nightmare of teeth, claws, and fear.

Nightmares had no place to be voiced here, however. She refused to even think of the werewolf haunting their dreams, because he had no right to be in their minds. Simple as that. She wouldn't give the creature any more power than it already had.

Standing up, she reached for the oil lantern and turned it brighter. "More light would probably do us all some good, don't you think?"

Eldridge nodded, still sitting on the ground and hugging his knees tight to his chest. On the other side of the lantern, Arrow also nodded. Even he wasn't getting up just yet. They both stared into the lantern with haunted expressions.

"Come on," she muttered. "The sooner we get this over with, the sooner we're out of this cursed place."

"I didn't know it would be like this," Eldridge whispered. "If I had known, I never would have brought you both here."

"Well, you wouldn't have gotten far without me. I would have followed you to the ends of the earth if you were going to save my mother." Freya reached out her hand for him to take and wiggled her fingers for his attention. "Stand up, Eldridge. We have a long way to go."

He looked up at her, eyes wide and brimming with tears. "I can't tell what's real and what's not, Freya."

"I'm real," she whispered. "As real as I was when I saved you from the Winter Court. I pulled you out of that prison and I will do it again if you need me to. But you have to stand first."

He stood, allowing her to draw him into her arms for a few moments. The hug cleared the dream from his thoughts, apparently. He pulled away from her and wiped an arm over his eyes. "Right. We have a long travel day ahead of us. Arrow, can you walk?"

The goblin dog stared straight ahead of himself, ears drooped down and tail tucked tight to his body. "I know that dream wasn't real. I know he wasn't really here, but those teeth..."

She met Eldridge's pointed look and nodded. Freya plucked the goblin from the ground and heaved him into her arms. "That's all right, Arrow. I'll carry you."

She had never guessed it would be this difficult just to walk through the mines. Something was in the air here, and all she could hope was that it wasn't the ore turning their minds insane. They still had to keep their wits about them if they were going to make it out alive.

Eldridge reached into his pocket and pulled out the tiny, glowing faerie. "It's time for you to go to work, my dear. I'd like to make a deal with you."

The power of the words laced through the air. And with all this strange magic swirling around them, she could almost see the power of his words. It swirled around him in a galaxy of color, blooming from his lips and wrapping around the jar. A few tendrils drifted off from the others, reaching for Freya before they returned to their master.

The will-o'-the-wisp pressed her hands against the glass jar. She nodded vigorously, listening to every word Eldridge said.

"Good." Eldridge held her jar up high to the light. "The Magician said you were bringing people to the werewolf's cavern. Is this true?"

She nodded again, pounding her fists on the glass.

"All right, then the deal is very simple if you follow the rules. I will let you out of this jar if you promise to take us to the werewolf's lair." He leaned close to the glass and glared at the tiny creature. "If you try to trick us, or if you don't bring us directly to the lair and try to lose us in this cursed place, then my magic will drag you right back to the jar wherever I leave it last. You will rot just like us in this cavern. Do we have a deal?"

Freya could see the tiny creature gulp. The fate would be worse than what would happen to them if the werewolf devoured their bodies. At least Freya and the others would be dead. This faerie would be trapped for all eternity.

Finally, the tiny faerie gave a sharp nod.

"Good enough for me," Eldridge snarled. "You made a deal with the Goblin King, wisp. Remember that."

Freya hoped the threat was enough to scare the faerie into actually guiding them correctly. Eldridge twisted the top of the jar and released the will-o'-the-wisp into the world.

She spun as she left her prison, stretching her arms over her head and coiling through the air like a ballerina. Every movement was graceful, and Freya could easily see why so many people would follow one of her kind into the darkness. The glittering brightness of her body and wings, the sheer joy in her expression, made Freya want to trust anything this creature said. Even though she knew how dangerous this little beast was.

The wisp turned around and gestured for them to follow her. And though they tried their best, it was difficult to follow something zipping so quickly. The faerie took a while to get her bearings, too. Though she'd been with them traveling, she had been stuck in Eldridge's pocket.

Every time the wisp darted down a tunnel, Freya's heart would jump in her chest. No one knew where they were going. This wisp was the only way to get them to the werewolf, and now she feared they would never get out again. The wisp wouldn't help them again, at least not without leading them to their death.

But she was shocked to see the wisp was actually showing them the right direction. They turned down a particularly narrow tunnel, and there was the cart they'd been looking for. Filled with mirror ore and a single gemstone seated on top the size of Freya's fist.

She glanced over at Eldridge and smiled. "I think we're getting somewhere."

"Ever closer." But his expression remained grim.

Freya didn't know if he was worried about what would happen when they found the wolf, or if he was concerned about the same thing as she was. How were they going to get out of this labyrinth?

They followed the wisp for what felt like hours before Freya noticed the veins in the walls. The silver mirror ore was stunning to look at, but it pulsed with magic like the power was blood flowing through the ore. Like the earth was alive, and these were actual veins the miners were ripping out.

She leaned a little closer to a particularly large chunk, watching as it pulsed again. Not with light. That only came from the lanterns both she and Eldridge held. The pulsing was the actual movement of the ore. Like it was liquid and not solid. It undulated within the walls.

"Eldridge?" she asked. "Are you seeing this?"

Freya straightened and realized her companions had wandered farther from her. Arrow had sat down in the middle of the tunnel nearest to her, and Eldridge leaned down to stare at another vein, much farther away from them.

But they were both frozen. Stuck in place like they didn't know how to move anymore.

Frowning, she called out again, "Eldridge?"

He didn't respond.

She left the ore she'd found and stumbled across the floor. Why couldn't she move her legs correctly? That was odd.

Staggering down the tunnel, she reached out her hand and braced her hand on the wall near Arrow. "What's going on, Arrow? I don't think I feel very good and I don't know why."

Her voice warbled, the same way it had when she had addressed the magic mirror. That should have meant something. A voice screamed in her head that the way she sounded was incredibly important, but she couldn't remember why. Or she couldn't focus on why. The thought danced out of reach like the glittering light of a wisp who was supposed to lead them through this madness.

She waved a hand through the shadows, slapping at the strange light bobbing in front of her eyes. She needed Arrow. He'd know what was going on.

Freya took one step, then fell onto her knees beside her faithful goblin companion. Squinting, she tried to touch his head, but it looked like he had four of them now. Which one was actually his head? It took her a few tries while her mind tried to focus on the sharp stones biting into her knees.

Finally, she set her hand on his skull and felt the soft fur of his ears underneath her fingers. "There you are," she whispered.

A blast of cold air trailed between her shoulder blades. She felt that thing inside her, the magic or power or whatever Eldridge had called it, unravel its wings. Suddenly, she saw herself and Eldridge further down the tunnel. They were walking away with their arms around each other, but Arrow's leg was stuck underneath a rock.

"Wait," he called out, his voice a hoarse croak. "Please! I'm right here. Don't you see me? I'm hurt!"

The image of herself and Eldridge did not stop. They looked at each other with glowing white eyes, kissed, and then walked on.

"No," Freya whispered. "No, my dear friend. We would never leave you."

But Arrow couldn't hear her. He was stuck in the vision of this nightmare and no matter how many times she called out to him, he never heard her.

Eldridge would know what to do. He could snap the goblin dog out of this horrible spell. All Freya had to do was get to him. Arrow might not be able to hear her, but Eldridge and her had a powerful connection. This wasn't the first time they'd conquered dark magic together.

She slapped her hands to the stone floor and pushed to stand. The long, grueling walk to his side was a staggering embarrassment. She fell onto her knees multiple times, crawling toward him with her hand outstretched. This was ridiculous. She knew how to walk, damn it.

Finally, she reached his side. And though she had to squirm on her belly to get there, Freya still reached out and wrapped a hand around his ankle. "Eldridge," she rasped. "We have to help Arrow."

But he didn't move. He stared into that ore and she already knew that something was horribly wrong. He was going to show her his own nightmare, and this time she didn't know if she would survive it. What was a Goblin King terrified of?

Mist poured off the ore he stared into. And then she saw a vision of herself down the hallway. Arrow wasn't in Eldridge's nightmare. A small blessing, she supposed.

Her image reached for Eldridge to take. "Come on!" she said, her voice strange and thin. "We're almost there! Just a few more steps and we'll finally save my mother."

How was this his nightmare? Did he not want her to find her mother?

Freya had worried about this. Eldridge had to know she would not leave him once she found her mother. Freya's life was here now, and even the woman who had birthed her wouldn't change that decision. Esther was here. Eldridge was here. All her new family and friends had made her life infinitely better in this place.

Then she saw those glowing red eyes again. They loomed out of the darkness behind her. Eldridge's image peeled out of his body, lunging for Freya in his vision.

He was too late.

The werewolf wrapped his jaws around her throat and shook his head once, twice, and the third time was enough. In a wild spray of blood, her head was removed from her shoulders. The werewolf kept the head in his mouth while her body dropped onto its knees, hands limp at her sides.

The sound that came out of Eldridge would haunt her for all eternity. A wild, keening cry of an animal in so much pain, she was certain he wouldn't survive it. He dropped onto his knees as well, that aching moan echoing over and over again.

With a gasp, she released her hold on his ankle. She couldn't watch that any longer without feeling her soul rip from her chest. She couldn't lose him like that, and he apparently couldn't lose her either. What a match.

She needed to get away from this ore or she'd be locked in this horrible dream state as well. What Freya didn't know was where to go. The ore seemed like it was everywhere.

Every tunnel she crawled past was filled with the silver stuff. She forced herself onto her knees, but that was no faster. She would drag her limp body and confused mind through this entire place until she finally grew too tired. And she was tired. So damned tired. All she had to do was lie down.

Perhaps she would die here alone, but wasn't that always going to be the case? Freya wouldn't have gotten out alive. She might have found the wolf, but her mother wasn't here anymore. And if she was, all she would have found were the bones that remained after the wolf had devoured her mother's corpse.

Freya had led her dearest friends into a trap. They would experience their worst nightmare over and over, and she would slowly rot away. Alone. Unloved. Forgotten by the world above.

Cold stone pressed against her cheek. When had she lied down? A stone pressed against her eye, a little too jagged and uncomfortable, but she couldn't move it. She couldn't move anything at all.

This was what she deserved. She should stay quiet, lay here, and wait for the inevitable.

Bright light flashed in front of her eyes. Bright, blue light that sparked a small nugget of hope in her chest.

The wisp. She was still here, somehow, and fluttering in front of Freya's face. Even as she struggled to open her eyes, the wisp was patting Freya's cheeks. Not quite as forceful as the dwarf, but enough to get her attention.

"I can't," Freya whispered.

The wisp flew back an arm's length, then launched herself at Freya's face. Her entire body slapped Freya's cheek, and that was enough to get her up. Freya lunged forward, sitting straight up and gasping in air.

This was just like the Spring Maiden's perfume. She knew how to get out of a situation like this. Hold her breath, stay cognizant of the world where she was. Though she didn't have those small buds to break open, she wasn't completely without tricks in this cavern.

She reached for the sharp stone that had dug into her cheek. With that in her palm, she stood. The overwhelming magic of the ore pressed down on her shoulders, but this time she dug the stone into the meaty flesh of her palm. The pain shocked her out of the trance.

"That'll do." She nodded at the wisp. "Lead on. Let's get out of here, and I'll come back for my friends."

And though it broke her heart to do it, Freya knew she couldn't snap them out of the daze they were in. The magic here was too powerful. All she could do was continue on.

She left a bloody trail in her wake, crimson droplets falling from her fist. If one of them woke before she returned to save them, perhaps they could still find her in this labyrinth.

CHAPTER 23

It took a long time to drag herself out of that tunnel. The wisp continued to come back and flutter in front of her face every time Freya started getting lost to the ore again. The bright, waving light was just enough to remind her that she needed to dig the rock into her hand again. Thus, Freya would.

And every time that pain zinged up her arm, she would force herself to take a couple more steps forward. Onward. Always onward until she burst out of the tunnel and fell onto her hands and knees.

Clean, fresh air filled her lungs. She could finally breathe without feeling like someone was holding her down. The magic released its hold on her reluctantly, but it had no choice.

Lifting her head, she stared at the strange place where the tunnels had spat her out. It was a field. She was kneeling in a field full of daisies of every color. Pinks, yellows, blues, whites, all dancing in a slight breeze that cooled the sweat slicking her skin. Green grass filled in the spaces between flowers, emerald in color and so lush it felt like her fingers were sinking into moss. And above all that color was a bright blue sky dotted with fluffy white clouds.

She had never thought that the mines would connect to a place like this.

Slowly, she stood. The flowers reached up to her knees, dancing as she stumbled forward. Freya tried her best to walk, but... why had the wisp brought her here?

The little faerie was nowhere to be found, either, so this must have been the right place. Unless the faerie had brought her to safety and the Goblin King's magic had sucked her back into the caves.

Freya doubted that was the case.

She walked into the center of the field and tilted her head back. The sun's rays played across her cheeks and the last remaining tension of magical control drifted away from her shoulders. She was free.

Dropping her head, she froze in shock. The werewolf stood at the edge of the field. His hands were held loose at his sides that heaved with great, powerful breaths. She thought he would run at her, teeth bared and slathering jaws open wide. She was in his meadow. This was the place where the wisp had brought people to die.

The werewolf didn't move.

He stared at her. She stared back at him, and Freya realized he wasn't going to move at all. The wolf was waiting for her to take the first step, and that was an intelligent response she hadn't expected.

Taking a step closer, she called out, "Hello!"

Any normal beast would have flinched at the sound of her voice. The wolves back home would have run the moment they heard a human shouting, and they wouldn't have stuck around to see what she wanted.

The wolf didn't react in any negative way. His ears flicked forward, and he tilted his head, but he stood there the same as before. Like he wanted her to keep talking.

She lifted her hands to show that she wasn't a threat, then

took another step forward. "I've been looking for you. Did you know?"

He moved his head in the slightest of nods.

"Good." She took a few more steps closer this time, testing to see how close he would let her get. "A pixie told me that you took my mother. She fought with you in the caves and when you beat her, you dragged her into the tunnels. No one has ever seen her again."

His ears twitched again. He nodded again, and Freya knew she was getting somewhere. This beast was not an animal. He knew what she was talking about. Who she was talking about. And this was the closest she'd ever gotten to finding her mother.

"Please don't run from me," she whispered. "I don't know who you are, or why you took my mother. But I need to find her."

The wolf turned away from her and headed off through the meadow. She felt her heart fall in her chest. She'd wasted her chance. Now the creature was running from her.

But the beast stopped and looked over its shoulder.

Did he want her to follow him?

Freya looked back at the dark mouth of the tunnel she'd left. Her companions were back there, caught in a nightmare and waiting for her to save them. It was the hardest choice she'd ever made. But she left them to follow the beast in the hopes she would return to this tunnel sooner rather than later.

She trailed the werewolf through the meadow, marveling as he fell onto all fours. It was easier for him to move like that, she thought. His back was hunched awkwardly, but he moved faster. Much faster.

Soon, she had to run to keep up with him. And what a strange feeling to be running through a meadow with a wolf at her side. They raced through the fields toward something she had missed until they were on top of it.

A mound of earth had been piled here. The flowers grew much thicker, creating a carpet of colors that led up to a small glass coffin. Inside, a very familiar woman laid with a bouquet of daisies clutched in her still hands.

The woman had cornflower curls laid out artfully around her head. She wore a blue overdress, the brass buttons that closed it at her shoulders still gleaming. Her white undergown hadn't aged a single day since her mother had left. It was the same outfit Freya remembered the last time she'd seen her mother. And she was the spitting image of Esther, just with a few years added to her life.

Freya gasped and felt her eyes fill with tears. "Mother," she whispered.

Some part of her had wondered if the wolf was her mother. She didn't know if the beast was male or female, she had simply assumed because of his broad chest. But now she could see with her own eyes. The beast was not her mother.

She stepped up to the coffin, nerves churning in her belly. She was irrationally afraid that her mother would open her eyes. And that was what Freya wanted more than anything. Proof that her mother wasn't lying in that coffin, dead.

But what would her mother say when she saw Freya had followed her into the faerie realm? Freya was terrified of her mother's disapproval. But Freya also knew her mother wouldn't open her eyes. After all, a coffin was only used to remember those who had passed.

Carefully, she set her fingers on the glass. Though she smudged it, the mark at least made her feel like this all was more real.

"My mother was an amazing woman and I love her very much," she said through thick tears. "Thank you for preserving her."

A blast of heat hit her back. The wolf had stepped too close, towering over her. She tensed, afraid he was about to put her in the coffin with her mother.

Instead, he tapped the glass over her mother's chest with his claw.

Her mother was still breathing.

Freya lunged forward again, pressing her hands to the glass and staring down at her mother with new eyes. "She's still breathing," she whispered as though she couldn't believe it. "She's alive."

The wolf nodded and moved. He stood on the other side of the coffin, awkward in nature but still clearly invested in whether or not her mother died.

He opened his muzzle and struggled through his words. "She... Sleep."

Freya frowned. Asleep? But that was magic only the Spring Maiden seemed to have.

She shook her head in disbelief. "I was placed under a similar spell before. The Spring Maiden was the one who made me fall asleep, and I couldn't wake up unless she let me."

Again, the wolf nodded. "Found in... mines. Curse hard... to break."

If he was suggesting what she thought, then that changed everything. It meant the Spring Maiden had not only lied to them, but she had willfully led them astray. She'd sent Freya, Eldridge, and Arrow after this wolf in the hopes that they would fix her problem while knowing she had caused Freya's greatest strife.

Where had all the air gone? Freya couldn't breathe.

She stepped away from the coffin and waved her hands in the air, counting all the reasons this didn't make sense. "So you're claiming all of this is the Spring Maiden's doing?"

The wolf nodded vigorously. He didn't move from where he was, but watched her with those all knowing red eyes. Those eyes that were so familiar because she had wanted them to be her mother's so desperately. Now, she realized this animal was just what the Spring Maiden said.

She pointed at him. "You're still a murderer. You've been hunting down pixies for how long? Killing them horribly. They find pieces of your victims and send them to the Spring

Maiden in the hopes she can cast some spell that would find you."

The werewolf looked at her mother, then back to Freya.

"I know she was put under a spell. What does she have to do with pixies?" Freya shouted the words. But then it dawned on her.

Of course he had been hunting pixies. They were the only way to get a message back to the Spring Maiden that what she had done was wrong. The werewolf wasn't a serial killer at all. He'd been trying to save her mother.

Frowning, she took a step closer to the wolf. "Did you want to kill the pixies?"

His eyes flashed bright red, and he bared his teeth in a snarl.

"Tell me," she insisted. "I need to know if you wanted to kill them, or if it was a message that you were sending to the Spring Maiden. Your answer changes everything, wolf."

He looked her dead in the eye and lifted both of his clawed hands. He gestured with the left, then the right, and finally brought his hands together, interlacing his fingers.

Freya sighed, disappointed at his answer. "They're one and the same, is that what you're saying? You wanted to send a message, and you wanted to kill them."

His snarling grin sent shivers of terror down her spine. Of course he had wanted to kill them. He was, after all, a wolf.

A memory bloomed in her mind's eye. Her father sitting beside her in front of their fireplace, cleaning his gun. He'd claimed all wolves were bad at their core. Some of them could wear sheepskin that would confuse people. They appeared good at first glance, but then they showed their true colors, eventually.

This wolf might be interested in her mother, perhaps because she was the first mortal he'd seen, but that didn't make him good. He was still a serial killer. Still the villain of this tale, even if she didn't want to believe that.

But there was the matter of what he'd done. He'd saved her

mother's life. He had taken care of her body even while she slept under a dreaming curse for all these years. And Freya couldn't forget that debt.

"She's my mother, and she means more to me than life itself." She looked at her mother's sleeping face and sighed. "For that, I am forever grateful. I don't think it's right to not give you something in return. What do you want?"

The wolf lifted his claws and pressed them against his heart. He then lifted them to the sky, then back to his chest once more.

"You want to live," she whispered. "Is that it?"

He nodded and took a step away from her. Away from the coffin as well. His eye darted to the vast landscape of the meadow, and Freya understood that bone deep desire that echoed through him.

The werewolf only wanted to be free. He didn't want anyone to hunt him as he let go of this strange, unusual job of watching over her mother's body. After all, a werewolf was a wild animal, and right now, he wasn't fulfilling that nature.

"Go," she said. "I won't know where you went. It will be hard to find you, but I suggest that you don't stay in the Spring Court. They're all watching you."

He pointed to her mother, a question in his eyes.

"I will look after her now. I give you my word that I will break this sleeping curse." Freya was surprised at the fervor in her own voice. "I vow it."

And with that, the wolf gave her a sharp nod, dropped onto all fours, and disappeared over the horizon.

CHAPTER 24

Freya made her way through the meadow back to the tunnel. Thankfully, she still remembered how to get back to that hidden place. It was a beautiful walk, enough to calm her mind and settle her back into the role she was most comfortable in.

Hero.

Freya knew what to do now that she was moving forward. She had a goal. Wake her mother and break the curse. She had a villain to defeat. The lying Spring Maiden, although she wasn't sure how the venomous woman had convinced them all she wasn't involved. These were tangible goals she could attack with reckless abandon.

But first, she had to get both Eldridge and Arrow out of the mines. Then they could work their magic and get all of them out of this meadow. Back to the Spring Maiden's castle, where she planned to wrap her hands around that skinny little neck and squeeze until the Spring Maiden's face turned purple.

Freya paused at the mouth of the cave. Already she could see the wisps of mirror ore magic reaching for her. This mine wasn't just dangerous. It should be sealed on both ends so no one would ever make the same mistake she and her companions had.

Someday she would return and make sure that happened.

"Wisp?" she asked, her voice echoing through the cavern. "Are you still there?"

It was a shot in the dark, really. She didn't expect the wisp to still be there. The tiny creature had done everything that she'd promised, and then some. She was the only thing that had gotten Freya through that nightmare.

No one responded.

She didn't blame the poor thing. The wisp had been in a jar for so many years, she likely wanted to go home. Or, at the very least, find whatever remaining family she had left in those mines.

That left Freya on her own, yet again. And she didn't have the faintest idea how to proceed this time. Was she supposed to plunge into the darkness? Her hand still ached from digging into the fleshy part of her palm with that rock. And she didn't have another sharpened object, so wouldn't she fall under the same curse?

She had no more tricks up her sleeve. All she could do was stare into the shadows and hear the Magician's words in her head.

"The question you should ask is if I'm human, not mortal."

That horrible old man had performed magic. And she'd done it before in the Winter Court, without thinking about it. That had to count for something. Freya had magic inside her. All she had to do now was figure out how to use it.

Taking a deep breath, she tried to remember what she'd felt in the Winter Court. The unknown man had approached them, the one who was now the Winter Prince. He'd walked up to them with confidence, and it wasn't that she had been afraid or nervous. She had just been tired. Freya hadn't wanted to deal with yet another faerie man who wanted to spit strange words and riddles at her. She'd wanted it all to be over.

Maybe that was the trick. She didn't have to bend the magic or know how to create some complicated spell. She had to give the control over to something else. Something she knew would take her away from this meadow and this madness.

Her next exhale flowed with power. The clean, crisp air from the meadow surrounded her. The breeze hugged her tightly, like a person was behind her. Even though she knew it wasn't a real person. It was magic. Magic that wanted her to know it was here with her and when she was ready, they could walk through the tunnel without fear.

She took a step into the darkness and waited for that horrible sensation of pressure on her shoulders. Instead, the wind she'd summoned from the meadow squeezed her shoulders gently and pushed her forward.

So she continued.

It was easy to walk this time. And when it grew too dark for her to see through the shadows, the wind brought her tiny daisies. They floated through the air. Some whole, some only petals. And they glowed with the most beautiful and delicate of light.

They illuminated the tunnel that had seemed so vast and unending when she first walked through it. But this place wasn't magic. Her mind had been under the influence of powers greater than her own. This was only a tunnel in the earth with gleaming silver ore embedded in the walls. That was all.

There was nothing to be afraid of in a place like this. The earth was magic, yes, but that magic could be manipulated into revealing what she wanted. Freya blinked and suddenly she could see lines in the floors. No, not lines, she realized.

Footsteps.

Singular imprints where she had walked before. They were close together, then staggering, then simply the dragging motion of her knees on the ground. But they were her footsteps and that meant she could follow them back to her companions.

"Thank you," she whispered.

The breeze swirled around her shoulders and filled her lungs with the sweet scent of spring. She remembered this scent from when her family had gathered sap every year. The air smelled like maple syrup and hope.

She took a deep breath and plunged through the darkness with more confidence than she'd felt in a long time. Eldridge wasn't that far, really. He was still frozen, staring at the wall with his eyes wide in horror.

How long had he been made to watch her die? And how many times had he relived that horror?

"Help him," she said as she put her hand on his shoulder. "No one deserves this."

The wind flowed down her arm and through their path in the tunnel. It wrapped around his shoulders, billowing fresh clean air into his lungs. Freya hoped it was enough to wake him. She desperately wanted to see those eyes open and watch as he recognized that she was standing right here in front of him, not wherever the image of her was.

"Eldridge," she said, calling out to him. "Eldridge, I'm okay. I'm right here."

His head tilted to the side, though his eyes remained trained on the ore.

She tried one more time, adding a little more lyrical quality to her voice. Cajoling him out of the nightmare. "You know I wouldn't be so foolish as to die in front of you. Goblin King. Come back to me."

Eldridge lifted his gaze from the ore and looked at her. She saw the hold of the ore's magic lift from his shoulders as if he was suddenly twenty pounds lighter. He heaved a sigh and then his eyes filled with tears.

He lunged for her, wrapping her in his arms so tightly she couldn't breathe. Repeatedly, he pressed his lips to her hair and whispered things that made little sense. "I'm so sorry. This was all my fault. I should have known what would happen. I'm sorry, Freya. No apology is good enough. My hero, my darling. My love."

The last word rocked through her entire being. She wrapped

her arms tightly around his waist and held him close to her heart. Tangled in his arms, she remembered what it was like to be so afraid that she would lose him. She remembered seeing him in that horrible prison in the Winter Court and in her nightmare when the werewolf had killed him. How could she not?

Freya was as afraid to lose him as he was to lose her.

Pressing her lips to his jaw, she drew back to kiss him. She lingered on the corners of his lips. The salt from his tears slid onto her tongue and she knew they were filled with love as well. So much love that they hadn't had the time to talk about yet. But they would. They had all the time in the world now.

"I need to get Arrow," she whispered, her throat closing with her own tears. "And you need to go back to the meadow. Follow my footsteps on the ground."

He didn't release her, but peered over her shoulder. "What footsteps?"

Had they already faded? That was annoying. Freya spread her fingers wide, feeling the tug of magic pulled from her navel. She didn't have to look behind her to know that the footsteps were glowing again. "The wind from the meadow is keeping the ore from tangling in your mind again. You won't fall under its spell as long as you follow in my footsteps."

"I won't leave you." He squeezed her tighter. "We stay together, Freya. That wolf is still out there."

She stared up into his horrified gaze and watched understanding dawn in his eyes. "He's not there, Eldridge. I already took care of it."

"You what?"

"Not everything is as it seems. You were the one to teach me that." She released her hold on his waist and forced him to let go of her shoulders. "I'll tell you when you get to the meadow, but I have to get Arrow out of this. You didn't see his nightmare. He... He..."

Eldridge shuddered and she could physically see the mantle of Goblin King descend. Though he wanted to remain with her, to wrap her in his arms, he understood the game of being the hero. The one who had to save everyone.

He took a step away from her, toward the footsteps, and nodded. "I know his greatest fear. He was abandoned as a child by his family, though they died tragically, it was still only him left. He fears that happening again."

"He does." Tears pricked in her eyes. "I can't let him suffer any longer, and I can't watch you at the same time."

He nodded again. Eldridge hesitated for a few more moments, his eyes sweeping her from head to toe as though he was checking one last time that she was alive and well. Then, the Goblin King turned and ran down the tunnel toward safety.

One down.

One to go.

Freya took a breath and continued. Arrow should only be a little distance away, but she was getting tired. Slogging through the ore's power felt like she was constantly moving through thigh deep snow drifts. She didn't know how much longer she could pull the wind with her.

There he was. A tiny black and white dog, curled up in a ball so tightly he looked a quarter of his size.

She lifted her hand and whispered, "Go."

The wind spread from her fingertips, gently wrapping around Arrow and weaving into his lungs. Freya picked him up in her arms. He didn't move. His body was so cold, she feared the worst, but whatever his horrible outcome, she knew she would never let him stay here in this tunnel.

He was hers, just as much as she was his. Their lives were intertwined now with so much love. He was her dearest friend, and she would do anything for him.

Step by painful step, she left the tunnel. Arrow stirred in her arms, his nose snuffling at her neck, before he lifted his head. "Freya?"

"Who else would it be?" she asked, turning around a corner and seeing light at the end of the tunnel.

"You came back for me." His voice was thick and tight with emotion. "I didn't know if you would."

"I never left you, Arrow. It was the magic, that's all. I had to go to the meadow to find the werewolf and put an end to all this." She smiled down at him and brought them both into the light. "It's already over. Now we only have a few loose ends to snip before this part of our story is complete. But know that we will end it together, as always."

The goblin dog wiggled in her arms and she put him down in the daisies. He lifted his nose into the air. His tail wagged happily, then he stood up on his back legs. "The sun is much better. The air here is..."

"Much better," she finished the sentence for him with a soft smile. "Now where is that Goblin King?"

She already knew where she would find him. It wouldn't take long for Eldridge to get his feet back under him, and the very first thing he would have done is explore this meadow. He'd want to make sure there was no danger to them. Namely in the shape of a werewolf.

Freya wandered through the daisies toward the coffin where her mother was laid to rest. And as it appeared on the horizon, the vision of a dark silhouette appeared, standing beside the glass where her mother lay.

"Is that..." Arrow cleared his throat. "That's not who I think it is, is it?"

"Yes, it's her." She tried very hard to not allow her voice to sound reverent, but... wasn't this a fairytale?

She'd listened to her mother tell her this story before. A woman who was waiting for true love's kiss, laid out in a field of daisies while resting in a glass coffin. This was the thing that stories were made of.

Stepping up to Eldridge's side, she put her hand back on the smudge she'd left before.

He was staring down at her mother with a frown on his face. "She's beautiful, Freya. You look very much like her."

Not really. Esther looked more like their mother, but she supposed there were a few similarities. She shared her mother's nose. There was that at least. They both had the angular features that her family shared. But that was where the similarities ended.

"I wish I looked more like her," she mumbled. "Esther favors our mother, though. If you had seen my father, you would have said I looked just like him. We were both lean and dark, while Esther and Mother always favored the light."

He put his hand on top of hers. His fingers were so much larger, stronger. "Where is the werewolf, Freya?"

"I let him go." She stared down into her mother's serene expression and wondered what Astrid would have done.

She probably would have killed the beast, regardless. Her mother wasn't one to let a faerie go just because it had saved someone else. All those lives of the pixies meant more than the single life of a mortal.

And yet... She couldn't kill the beast. Freya had to give him a chance.

"You let him go?" Eldridge repeated, stunned. "Why would you do that?"

"He was keeping her safe. She went into the mines. But I don't think he was killing pixies back then. She fell under this spell while they were meeting and he tried to protect her. He recognized the spell that was laid on her and he put her here." She turned her hand around and laced their fingers together. "He kept her alive in the hopes that someone would come to collect her someday. I had to let him go."

Tiny lines appeared between Eldridge's eyes. "A sleeping spell, you say?"

"Just like what the Spring Maiden did to me." Finally, she met his gaze without flinching. "I don't know why she lied to us, but this is all her doing. She put my mother to sleep, just like she did me. And then she sent us to kill the beast who was trying to force her to recognize her own mistakes."

He let out a low growl. "Then I think we need answers from the Spring Maiden."

Arrow stepped up and placed his paw on top of their hands. "She's the only one who can wake your mother. The sleeping spell she uses is one she thought up on her own. The flowers you saw, Freya. Those might be the key."

Freya looked at her companions and realized how lucky she was to have them. Together, they could overcome any obstacle.

She straightened her spine and squared her shoulders. "I suppose it's time for us to take down yet another faerie noble, gentlemen."

CHAPTER 25

It was easier to say they were going to take down the Spring Maiden, than actually doing it. Their plans took over an entire afternoon and then spread into the next night. A day turned into much longer as they paced through the meadow.

Eldridge summoned food and water for them. They could have portaled into the Spring Court, but that would get them nowhere. The Spring Maiden had planned all of this in detail, thus she likely would know they had found her out.

She was sacrificing her own people to a monster. But why? It made little sense. Nothing about this added up and Freya wanted to understand before they went on the attack.

Her two companions were more than happy to rip apart every step of their journey. They hashed out every detail that the other might not have been a part of. They told their story a hundred times over, pouring details into each other's head. But no matter how many times they rehashed what had happened, everyone landed on the same thing.

This didn't add up.

The Spring Maiden had never cursed someone where she couldn't look into their heads. She had certainly never let one of her dreamers escape from the Spring Court. So why was Freya's mother different?

Freya had taken to sitting next to her mother's coffin. Eldridge had summoned a small stool out of thin air, so Freya sat and braided little flower crowns like her mother had taught her so long ago. The repetition of moving her hands helped ease her mind.

"Why were you here?" she asked every day. "You hated the faerie realms. You hated these people and yet you were here. The Spring Court is the worst of them all, so why, Mother?"

If only she would wake. Then Freya could ask her a thousand questions. Her mother had always helped her to see the world in a different light.

"Did you want to find more books?" she asked. She had found the chest in their garden. That was how Freya had gotten into the faerie realm to begin with.

But again, she hadn't entered the magical realms in the Spring Court. Freya had been spit out into that in-between place. That world between the realms, not here. So how had her mother traveled so far?

And then there was Eldridge. He'd said he loved her, or as good as said it. She didn't know how many times he'd been hinting at it, but whatever the hints, she now felt a little strange being around him. Not uncomfortable per say, but like her heart was going to burst if she didn't say it back.

She wasn't ready to say it. But he'd said that he loved her, so shouldn't she say something back? At least to reassure him that his affections were reciprocated. But she didn't know how to say she was in love with a creature her mother had trained her to hate.

The flower in her hand fell apart in her tight grip. Damn it. Now she was going to have to find another flower to replace this one, and she didn't want to leave her mother's side while she was feeling so... so...

A wet nose pressed against her wrist with the perfect flower held between his teeth. "Miss Freya, you can use this one."

Though the words were garbled, the meaning was still behind them. Of all people, Arrow would always be the one to take care of her.

"Thank you," she said. The flower stem was the perfect length to weave into the last piece of this flower crown made of entirely white daisies. A rarity in this field. "I think this one is going to be my best yet."

"Well, you have a whole stack of them to choose from." Arrow looked at the dozens of crowns strewn around her mother's coffin. "Are you all right, Freya? You don't seem like yourself."

"I don't think I've been myself since I came here." She sighed and set the crown down in her lap. "When I struggled with my first quest, it was a time when I had to defy everything I had learned. I had to suspend disbelief and realize magic was real. Then I had to go to the Winter Court and save Eldridge, finding out that I have magic too. And here... Here I have become something different. Someone different. I hardly recognize myself and I don't know where to go from here."

He set his head on her knee and sighed. Arrow stared at her mother with those big, sorrowful eyes. "I don't think there's an answer to what you want, Freya. We're all changing. And no mortal comes to the faerie realm without being affected by the magic. Look at your sister!"

But she didn't think it was the magic that had changed her. Nothing about the way she had manipulated the wind made her feel like she had changed in this place. She'd pulled on something deep inside her very soul to do it. And that power felt like it had been there for a very long time, waiting for her to use it to communicate with this realm.

She shook her head. "I don't know. I don't know why all of this is happening now when my mother would have stopped at nothing to make sure it never developed."

In the reflection of her mother's coffin, she saw Eldridge step toward them. He was every inch the Goblin King. His perfectly pressed suit. His handsome features, silver skin glowing in the light. The wind ruffled the tufts of fur on the tips of his ears.

"Your mother may have been protecting you," he said. "Magic in the mortal realm will get you killed. That is the danger of being like us."

"Like us?" she repeated. Freya stared up at him with wide eyes. "I'm not fae, Eldridge. You know that. I'm just a mortal woman, like my sister and my parents. Nothing about me is different except this... this..."

"Magic." He said.

The Goblin King sank down beside Arrow. All three of them turned their attention to her mother's coffin. Perhaps it was easier for them to look at the sleeping woman rather than each other.

Freya struggled to talk about this. She wasn't different, and yet she was. Every fiber of her being wanted to shout that she hadn't changed because she was so afraid that her mother would wake up and not like what she saw.

Freya had always been the good, dutiful daughter. She was the image her mother had wanted to create. A capable woman who never touched magic. No matter the cost.

Now, if her mother woke and saw her daughter using magic... What would she do? Would she lose her family all over again when she had only just found her?

A groan escaped her lips. Freya folded over her legs, pressed her arms to her knees, and held her head in her hands. What was she supposed to do?

Eldridge touched the back of her head and pressed his lips to her hair. "My darling, we will handle this together. I know there is so much you fear, but we cannot do anything until we wake your mother."

"I know," she whispered. "This would all be so much easier if I wasn't so frightened of what she will say when she sees me."

"Perhaps you should be more frightened of what the Spring

Maiden will say." He drew her back up to sitting, a smile on his face. "Focus on the first obstacle, and then we will continue our story from there."

The first obstacle. She could do that.

Freya steadied herself and tried to remember this was what she had wanted. An opportunity to put her family back together. And Eldridge was right. They could do nothing about how her mother would feel about Freya's choices until she was actually awake.

The Spring Maiden would have to do that. And the rage Freya had originally felt that the horrible faerie noble had taken advantage of her family needed to fuel her.

She closed her eyes and let that anger flow through her entire body. Heat blasted through her veins, warming her to the very core because she knew now was the time for her to rise to the occasion. The Spring Maiden was in the dark, and that was because, like all the other faerie court leaders, the Maiden had underestimated Freya.

"I don't think she even thought we'd make it this far," Freya said. She squeezed her eyes tighter. "She sent us here because she thought the werewolf would kill us. Two birds with one stone and all that."

"Perhaps." Eldridge took her hands and squeezed them tight. "Or perhaps she thought that she could get us out of the way until she completed whatever this was supposed to do for her. Perhaps it has something to do with your family line."

Her family was no more special than the average mortals. But it didn't make sense that the Spring Maiden would target her mother. It didn't...

"Gah." She abruptly opened her eyes and stood. "I need to speak with the Spring Maiden or all these possibilities are going to drive me mad. How do we get there?"

"We don't without a plan." Eldridge stood as well. "Do you have a plan, Queen Killer?"

He knew how much she hated that name. Glaring, she shook

her head. "No. I don't have a plan. And I don't think we need one."

Her two companions shared a look, then Arrow asked, "Come again?"

"The Spring Maiden likely thinks we're dead already. Isn't that how this should have worked out? We find the werewolf. He kills us. We never know about my mother at all." She pointed off in the direction the werewolf had run. "She didn't anticipate the werewolf still having his wits about him. I don't know why he gave me the chance to talk with him, but he wanted to explain himself. There was humility in his eyes, Eldridge. He was not a monster. She needs to answer not only for my mother, but for him. Right now, we have the surprise advantage."

He tapped his chin with a long finger. "Or she might be expecting us to rush back, and this was all some elaborate ruse. She may know we'll run back to her court and that's where the real trap lies."

"No." Freya refused to believe that. "She's not that crafty. She always thinks she has the upper hand."

And in this case, she didn't. Freya would catch her off guard and then they would question the Maiden. Now, they had to find a way to get into the Spring Court without anyone seeing them.

She narrowed her eyes on Eldridge. "Did you leave anything in our private room so we could teleport back to it easily?"

His eyes widened in shock. "How did you know that's how I teleport?"

Well, that was an awkward question. She hadn't really known at all. At least, he'd never told her such a thing. Had she been using magic to get that answer? Freya didn't know.

Instead of wondering if she'd somehow crossed yet another line, she shrugged. "Does it matter? I need to know if we can teleport into the castle with my mother. I want to hide her. Leaving her here is leaving our best bargaining tool behind. Besides, I don't trust the Spring Maiden not to try to move her again."

At least he didn't try to argue with her. Eldridge gave a sharp nod and reached out his hand to place it on the coffin. "Do you want the entire thing moved, or just her body?"

The awful question was the first of many, she was sure. Bringing an entire coffin was bound to get tricky. So she leaned down and pushed off the lid. The same as the Winter Princess had done all those months ago.

The glass hit the ground but didn't shatter. A loud thunk was all it made before it settled in the daisies.

Her mother was within reach. Freya shouldn't feel like she was looking at a dead body, but she did. With a shaking hand, she touched her fingers to her mother's warm cheek. "We're going to wake you up, Mother. I promise."

Eldridge winced and placed his own hand on her mother's shoulder. "Everyone touch me. Teleporting isn't easy and I want us all there in one piece."

Freya reached out, grabbed onto him, and squeezed her eyes shut. It was time to confront a faerie noble.

Yet again.

CHAPTER 26

They landed within their room in the castle, a little harder than Freya would have liked. She stumbled to the side. Frantically, she searched for her companions and was relieved to find Eldridge holding her mother in his arms.

"Is she all right?" she asked.

"She's still asleep if that's what you want to hear." Eldridge carefully laid her mother in the gilded bed. Flowers had grown in the canopy in their absence. White roses rained petals down on her mother's head. They lingered in her hair, tangling through the golden curls.

"She looks like a princess," Freya murmured.

"There have been many princesses in the same predicament." Eldridge rounded the bed to pull her into his arms. "And they all woke up, I'm happy to say."

Arrow grunted. "All the ones you know about. I'm sure there's still some in those beds."

"Arrow!" Both Freya and Eldridge scolded at the same time.

"What?" He trotted toward the door. "I was just saying what everyone was thinking."

Freya rolled her eyes as Arrow pressed his ear to the wood. Sure, he meant well. But she didn't want to hear about how there were many others still trapped by the Spring Maiden's magic. She would wake her mother up. No matter what the cost.

Stepping out of Eldridge's arms, she looked between the two of them. "Arrow, would you mind staying here with my mother? Just to make sure no one comes in and tries to steal her."

He pulled away from the door and rolled his eyes. "I know you're trying to keep me out of trouble. What am I going to do if a pixie walks in to get your mother? Hmm?"

He'd seen right through her plan.

Freya cleared her throat and asked, "Bite them?"

"Right. Because they'd be so afraid of a dog bite." But he still hopped up onto the bed and curled up next to her mother's feet. "Fine. That's fine. Leave the goblin dog because he doesn't have any magic. I see how it is."

"That isn't the only reason and you know it." She knelt and hugged him tightly around the neck. "I'm sorry, but I need you to stay. I don't know what the Spring Maiden might throw at us, and I can't keep track of both of you. At least I know she won't be inclined to attack the Goblin King. But you? If she had her way, I'm certain she would try to harm you because you mean so much to me."

He grumbled but at least seemed appeased.

And she now knew someone was watching over her mother, which was a small blessing. If the Spring Maiden tried to move her mother's body, then she'd have to move Arrow, too. And Freya knew she could find Arrow no matter what.

She reached for Eldridge and took his hand. "Time to find the Spring Maiden?"

"It's time." He dragged her out the door.

Together they raced through the halls until they found the servant's exit that he'd taken her out last time. Eldridge slowed down in front of the door, squeezing her fingers tight and watching her with wide eyes. "Are you sure you're ready for this?"

"I defeated the Winter Princess, didn't I?" Somehow, that felt a lot harder than what she was about to do. Sure, the Spring

Maiden was terrifying. But she wasn't nearly as powerful as the witch who had become the Goblin Queen.

This was easy compared to the creatures she'd beaten before. Even if the Spring Maiden didn't believe it.

Freya put her hand on the door as if she could feel the powerful creature beyond it. "I don't intend on fighting her, Eldridge. We're not going to waltz in there and throw spells or brandish swords. I want to reason with the Spring Maiden first. Like I wanted to with the Winter Princess."

He nodded, albeit slowly. "We'll play this one by your rules then, Freya. I trust your judgement."

Now, she just hoped she was right.

Freya pushed the door open and walked into the gardens beyond. There were countless pixies all pruning the flowers. Some were up trees, trimming the blossoms that fell to the ground and filled the air with a sweet, apple blossom scent.

She counted twenty pixies within eyesight, and that meant the Spring Maiden had more back up than Freya wanted her to have. The pixies all had sharp teeth and wings. They could easily overcome both her and Eldridge.

She had to be certain the Spring Maiden was caught off guard and didn't order her many pixies to attack.

Leaning over to Eldridge, she muttered, "Can you freeze these pixies when I tell you to give us some privacy?"

He glanced around at them, seemingly counting each and every opponent. "There's not that many of them. I should be able to do it, but if anyone walks into the fray, then they won't be frozen."

"That's fine. I don't think I'll need that long to convince her." Freya found the Spring Maiden in the middle of all the pruning.

The lovely lady of this court sat at a delicately made table and chairs. The twisted metal was painted bright white, and a tea set sat on top. Beautiful porcelain gleamed as white as the table, with tiny yellow flowers painted all over it. The Spring Maiden sipped from the smallest teacup Freya had ever seen.

And she was alone.

Perfect.

"Give us a little privacy, Eldridge." She narrowed her eyes on her prey. "I think the Spring Maiden and I should have a talk."

Freya relied on surprise being her only weapon. She had nothing but her own wits about her, but that should be enough. Where the Winter Princess loved battle and showing her teeth, the Spring Maiden only wanted to be regarded as powerful.

She didn't actually have the ability to be powerful herself. Not really.

Every pixie in the garden froze at the same time. Eldridge's magic didn't touch the Spring Maiden, and it took the noble faerie a few moments to realize her subjects weren't moving.

The Spring Maiden frowned as Freya took a seat opposite her on the table. "Hello," Freya said. "It's been a while since you and I talked. Hasn't it?"

The teacup fell from the Maiden's hand and shattered on the table. A soft whimper escaped her lips, and she looked down at the mess she'd made. "My goodness, that's hot tea. You should stay away from that mess, my darling. Your delicate hands would get scalded."

"Would they?" Freya reached forward and caught the Spring Maiden's hand. "I think you're stalling. You didn't expect me to be back so soon, did you?"

"Or at all," the Maiden grumbled.

Freya bristled. This woman wasn't even trying to hide the fact that she hadn't wanted Freya or her companions to return. And though she knew the fae couldn't lie, Freya had hoped that the Maiden would at least pretend to be a little remorseful.

Instead, what she got was a woman who cared very little that Freya was here and struggling. The Maiden didn't even feel guilty for what she had done and all the people she had harmed along the way.

Freya clutched the side of the table until her palms ached. She could not let herself fly into a rage, nor could she launch over this table and grab the Spring Maiden around the neck. That was what she had told Eldridge that she didn't want to do. Fighting would only get them so far, and that progression would be nothing compared to what diplomacy would do.

She couldn't repeat what happened in the Winter Court. Freya wasn't sure she would survive it.

The death of the Winter Princess weighed on her mind even now. Which was why she was so settled on giving this faerie a chance. "You knew my mother was under your own spell. I want to know why."

"So you found her, then?" The Spring Maiden reached for Freya's teacup and shakily brought it to her lips. "How odd. I didn't think you would find her at all."

"Yes, I did. And I found the wolf as well, who was quite adamant that he wasn't the monster you painted him to be." Freya leaned forward and narrowed her eyes. "You knew he was sending you dead pixies as a way to ask for help, didn't you?"

The Spring Maiden's hand was shaking so badly, she had to put down the teacup. It clattered against the metal table and she immediately waved for one of her servants to come over.

Freya had already suspected this would be the Maiden's plan. Freya knew she would try to get out of this conversation, disappearing into the morning mist. The woman was less confrontational than any faerie she'd met in her travels.

When no servant appeared, the Maiden licked her lips. "Of course. You have Eldridge helping you."

"I don't need anyone's help to stop you. I want that to be very clear." Freya bared her teeth in a snarl. "Or have you forgotten my new name? Your people call me the Queen Killer for a reason."

"The Winter Princess let you kill her. Or you had help from Eldridge the same way you did when you beat him." The Maiden's face turned bright red. These words weren't lies. They were what she wanted to believe. "You are still just a mortal woman and one such as you could never defeat the Spring Maiden. Not for good."

Freya tilted her head and watched the Maiden's expression slowly shift into one of fear. "You know that's not true. Otherwise you never would have gone to such lengths to hide the truth from me. So what is it really, Maiden? I'm giving you a chance to not end up in the same place as the Winter Princess. I don't want to kill you. Despite all the flaws I saw in that horrible mining town, I believe you love this Court. And that, given the right tools, you could fix all the wrongs here."

She honestly wasn't sure that the Spring Maiden could. And she was surprised to realize that she wanted to give the woman a chance. After all the Maiden had done, Freya still believed the Spring Maiden could be better than the other fae.

Dahlia was more fierce than the others. And though she loved luxury, her own castle was the truest to her season. Beautiful on the outside, but deadly on the inside. The Spring Maiden wanted to let that side of herself emerge. That darkness wanted to be free and to rule as she should, rather than how other people expected her to.

And that was the chance Freya grasped.

The Spring Maiden looked at Freya, then glanced around them. Clearly searching for Eldridge. "I don't know what you're talking about, my dear. The werewolf has hunted us for generations. Your mother was in the wrong place, at the wrong time. That's why I told you she was here. There's no hidden meaning behind my words. I'm not hiding anything from you."

The lies must have burned. And Freya watched with pleasure as the Maiden's face turned green. The faerie pressed a hand to her stomach and the other to her mouth as she held in the vomit from the lie.

"You want to purge yourself of those words, don't you?" Freya asked.

The Maiden glared.

"I know your kind can't lie, and this is the price you must pay for trying to do so." Freya leaned back in her chair and looked at the dirt underneath her nails. Anger simmered just underneath the surface of her skin, and she felt that age old confidence rise inside her. The magic that had been passed down through her blood. "I can make you tell me, you know."

"Well, that would be a trick to have a mortal forcing a fae to do anything."

Freya lifted her hand and squeezed her fingers in the air. Like she was choking the Maiden as she so desperately wanted to do. Eyes wide, the Maiden reached up and touched her throat.

The air twisted between Freya's fingers. Almost like it gave her the semblance of what the Maiden's neck would feel like. She squeezed a little tighter.

"It's not a trick," Freya hissed. "But I think you know that. Why else would you keep my mother locked away? You know something I don't. Last chance, Maiden. I have no interest in playing around. I'm sure there are more people in this realm that know what you know. So spit it out, or I will move on to the next person to question."

Eyes wide, the Maiden slapped at her throat until Freya released her. Long wheezes echoed from the Maiden's lungs as she gasped in air.

Freya patiently waited until the Maiden could breathe again. Then she raised her brows.

"I always suspected," the Maiden rasped. "I never thought it could be true. Your mother was meddling with things no mortal had any right to look at. She was obsessed with magic while remaining entirely human. When she came into this realm, I thought it better to put her to sleep rather than allow her to find more faerie secrets."

"That's it?" Freya shook her head in denial. "That's not the entire story."

The Maiden bared her sharpened teeth. "Your whole family was cursed. The more I looked into it, the more I feared what your story truly was. Your father, your sister, even you. Everyone was touched by magic and you never should have been. Mortals living in the mortal realm with magic? No. That's never allowed."

"So you put my mother to sleep?" Freya furrowed her brow. Pieces were missing from this story. "What about my father?"

"I never met the man."

"But you must know where he is. If you had my mother, then he wouldn't be far behind." Freya said the words hesitantly, however, because she wasn't so sure.

No one had been in that meadow with her mother. And Father would never have let her mother remain in that state. She would have been less surprised to find him dead, draped over her mother's coffin. But not there at all? That was suspicious.

The Spring Maiden swallowed hard. "I have told you everything I know. Your father was not with your mother when she arrived in the Spring Court."

Freya wanted to deny it. But there was always more to a story, no matter how much she wanted this to be the end. "You'll wake her now."

"No," the Maiden said, then frowned. "I will not wake her until we find out why she was here. Why she was cursed. You were supposed to help with the werewolf, and obviously you were sidetracked."

"I took care of your werewolf problem. That was the deal, and I upheld my end of the bargain." Freya stood and leaned over the table, her nose nearly touching the Maiden's. "Now we're making another deal, and you're going to take it. You wake up my mother and I will let you live. If you refuse one more time, then you will join your sister in her icy grave."

The Maiden's eyes widened.

"Yes. I don't plan to bury you here when I'm done with you." Freya cupped the Maiden's cheek and tried to smile in the same feral way as the other always did. "I'm not so kind as to let you stay in your home, even after death. It's your choice, Maiden. But I don't think you question whether or not I can actually do this. I think you know if I wanted to end your life, then I could. With just the snap of my fingers."

The Maiden swallowed hard, then slowly nodded. "I'll wake your mother when we're finished here."

"Now."

"I can't..." The Maiden's eyes darted left and right, then she relented. Her shoulders curved in on herself and she looked very small. "Now. As you request."

"Good." Freya straightened and patted the other woman's shoulder. "And in thanks, once I find my mother alive and well where I have left her body, I will ensure the Goblin King sends you more assistance. Your people need you. And despite all this, I still believe you are the one who can help this court."

Freya left the Maiden sitting where she was and joined her Goblin King on the other side of the castle.

Heart pounding in her chest, Freya met Eldridge's questioning gaze and said, "It's done. Let's see if my mother's awake."

CHAPTER 27

Her stomach churned with every step up the stairs. Freya had thought if she ever got the chance to reunite with her mother, that she would be intensely excited. She'd expected to run up the stairs and throw the door open with love and hope in her heart.

But all she felt was fear. What if her mother didn't recognize her? It had been years.

And what if her mother was disappointed? There was no getting around the fact that Freya was in the faerie realms, as her mother had always told her not to do. And she certainly couldn't explain away the Goblin King. Or the goblin dog, who was likely sitting on the bed with her mother right now.

She scratched the back of her neck and stared up at the ceiling, stopping at the top of the stairs. "Hang on," she muttered. "I need a few minutes."

Eldridge paused as well. He put a hand on her back and rubbed the tension between her shoulder blades. "What is it? I thought you'd want to see your mother as swiftly as possible?"

"I thought so, too." But she couldn't breathe. Every muscle in her body locked up tight and her thighs quaked with fear.

Her mother was going to be so disappointed that Freya had

done everything in her power to go against what she'd been taught. She was not only in the faerie realms, but she'd fallen in love with the enemy. One of the dreaded creatures who... who...

She looked up into Eldridge's eyes and realized she couldn't even think such dark thoughts any more. Oh, she loved him more than anything in the world. She'd even give up her family for him, if he asked her to. It wouldn't be easy. And it would feel like ripping her own heart out of her chest. But she would do it.

Eldridge was more important than anyone else now.

Tears burned her eyes. Freya launched herself at his chest and wrapped her arms around him. "I'm not going anywhere," she whispered against his shirt. "No matter what she says. I don't want to go anywhere. I want to be with you wherever you are."

"Oh, Freya," he replied with a chuckle. Eldridge held her tightly against his heart. "I never worried about that. You're a grown woman and you've proven yourself more than capable in my world. Who else could have saved your mother from the clutches of a sleeping spell? She would have been there for all eternity if you hadn't done something about it."

"None of that will change her opinion on you or your kind." Maybe that's what she was worried about. Freya wanted him to be happy and to fit in with her family. Like the man she'd always thought she would end up with. But the problem was that Eldridge wasn't that man.

He was a goblin. A terrifying, monstrous creature who her parents would have hated.

Would hate.

It was hard to start thinking about her mother in the present tense. The woman was waiting for her disappointing daughter, Arrow probably talking her ear off, and Freya didn't even think she could walk inside.

Pulling back, she sniffed loudly while trying to keep the tears from falling. "Do you think we should get Esther first?"

"And leave your mother in the Spring Court for even longer?"

He rolled his eyes. "Freya, I think you're stalling. Your mother can't be all that bad."

She thought back to the countless times Astrid had struck Freya over the knuckles for even daring to question her teachings. How many times her mother had scolded her for daring to think that the fae could maybe be a little more complicated than just bad.

And she remembered how her mother had warded their property like a mad woman, insisting that no faerie ever step foot on their property because they were horrible creatures with nightmarish features.

"No," Freya replied, her voice soft and brows furrowed. "She can't be that bad, I suppose."

Releasing her hold on the only person who felt like a lifeline, Freya turned back to the hallway that would lead her to her mother. Had it gotten longer since they left? It sure seemed like it took a thousand steps before she stood in front of the door she had to open.

Freya froze. She didn't want to open the door. She didn't want to see her mother when she knew what the other woman would say.

That Freya had disappointed her.

She'd fallen into the same pit as Esther, and in doing so, had become a shame to their family name.

Her fear was valid and true. It shook through her very core and trembled down to her bones. Freya put her palm on the door and listened quietly.

Screaming was to be expected. Her mother would shout at Arrow, then likely try to attack him. The goblin dog would not bite her mother, so she wondered if maybe he was harmed in the battle.

But when she pressed her ear to the door, she didn't hear any of that. All she heard was the quiet murmuring of a soft conversation on the other side. A conversation that sounded nothing like what she would have expected from her mother.

Eldridge put his hand on her back once again. "Freya. I promise you that nothing is going to go wrong. But if we want to understand what is happening, then we have to talk with your mother. Don't you think?"

She did, but that didn't make it any easier.

Sighing, she replied with nothing more than a firm nod. Flexing her fingers on the wood, she nudged it open.

The hinges swung open to reveal her mother sitting up on the bed. White rose petals still tangled in her blonde hair, although now her eyes were open. She stared at Arrow, who sat at the foot of the bed like a normal dog would. Perhaps to keep her at ease. He was talking though, and that would be the first indication that he wasn't entirely an animal.

Her mother was cross legged, hands resting on her knees, and for all purposes looked rather calm. When the door opened, she looked at them with kind, intelligent eyes that didn't immediately flare with rage when she saw Eldridge behind her daughter.

Freya didn't know what to do. Did she walk into the room? She felt a bit like an intruder who had interrupted an important conversation that she had no right to interrupt.

In contrast, her mother immediately stood and rounded the edge of the bed. Astrid paused ten feet from her daughter, watching every movement with wide eyes that brimmed with tears.

"My girl," her mother choked. "I never thought I'd see you again. Look how much you've grown."

"Well, it's almost been ten years." Freya suddenly realized how angry she was. So angry she was shaking.

She needed an explanation.

Freya and Esther had been alone for too long. They had struggled through life because their parents had disappeared without a single word of warning, and now she found out that they were alive? How many years of her life had she given up to become her mother, when the woman was still here?

Freya ground her teeth and tried so hard not to let the venomous words slip off her tongue. She glared at the woman who dared to be happy to see her.

Astrid took a step back and shook out her hands at her sides. "I suppose I have a lot of explaining to do."

"More than that," Freya snarled. "You were here? You told us to never go to the faerie realms, no matter what happened. I came here to get Esther back and now I find you've been here the whole time? Why? Where is Father? What were you doing in the Spring Court of all places?"

A thousand questions spilled from her lips and she knew that her mother wouldn't answer them all. But she wanted to advance on the older woman, spitting angry words and bitter heartbreak that she'd suffered since her mother had left.

A daughter deserved her mother's attention, time, and love. Freya had suffered without it for too long and that space where her love had once been, now filled with anger.

"I'm sorry," her mother replied. "I know it's not enough."

"No, it's not." Freya turned toward the fireplace. It was the only spot in the room where she wouldn't have to look at her mother.

The clicking of dog paws hitting the ground didn't make anything better. Arrow trotted over in front of her and sat down hard on the floor. He glared up at her as only her dearest of friends could do. "Your mother has a lot to tell you."

"I'm sure she does. But now that she's awake, I'm not so sure I really care to hear it." Freya looked beyond him, back toward the fireplace. "She can speak with Esther if she needs additional help. Considering she was here, I assume she was looking for something in the faerie realms."

"Freya." Her mother touched her shoulder. "This is something you need to hear as well, my darling. You have every right to be mad at me. There just isn't enough time for us to have this argument."

That anger boiled in her chest. She should control it. Contain it. Be the daughter her mother wanted her to be.

Snarling, she whipped around and threw her mother's hand off her shoulder. "We don't have time? Do you know how much time I had sitting in that cottage, waiting for you to come home? I was fourteen!" Freya dashed at the tears in her eyes. They weren't helping. "I didn't know how to take care of a child, let alone myself. I wanted my mother to come home. My father to protect us. Instead, I had to grow up. I had to be the one to everything for Esther and myself!"

"I know!" her mother shouted. "Do you think I'm unaware of what I put my daughters through? There wasn't any other option for your father or I."

"No other option?" Freya screamed the words back.

How dare her mother even suggest that? There was always another choice when children were involved. Hands shaking, she lifted them in the air and pretended she didn't see the way the furniture in the room rattled against the floor.

Every angry retort and frustrated argument rose from deep within her soul. She hadn't realized just how much hatred and anger had built in the absence of her mother, but here it all was. All rising to the surface at the same time.

She had been abandoned by the one person who should have stayed.

Power rippling through her voice, Freya growled, "You could have brought us with you. Every other choice would have been better than what we suffered through. I made sure Esther lived, and I did everything you said. I sacrificed everything because you couldn't be a good mother and stay with your children."

She had thought the bitter, angry words would make her mother argue all the more. She'd been that kind of woman when Freya knew her. Even the thought of her daughter's rebelling had made Astrid punish them.

And here she was. Silently watching her daughter rage,

clearly using magic when that should have made her mother even more angry.

Instead, Astrid stood in the center of the room and let her daughter expel all that awful energy. Her face was calm as the glass of a magic mirror.

When Freya finished yelling, Astrid took a step forward and cupped her daughter's face in her hands. "Your father is the werewolf, Freya. The same one you hunted. Arrow informed me of the quest given to you by the Spring Maiden. We were both hunting the same quarry, but for different reasons."

The words echoed through her head.

Her father was the werewolf.

She'd been hunting the only man who had been her support structure. Her kind-hearted father with soulful eyes and a skill for music.

He was a werewolf.

Freya realized Eldridge had caught her by the elbows and was lowering her into one of the chairs by the fireplace. But she couldn't focus on the surrounding world when her mother had ripped the floor out from under her feet.

Her father couldn't be a werewolf. There were no werewolves in the mortal realm, not anymore. Hardly any werewolves even lived here, in the faerie realms.

"How?" she muttered. "How is that possible?"

Astrid sank to her knees before her daughter, placing her palms on Freya's legs. "He wasn't always like this. The incident happened after you and Esther were born, you see. He had come from the faerie realm. Not a fae, but a changeling child. It's... complicated. But, he went back to see his family and when he returned, there was a wound on his shoulder. We had hoped the curse wouldn't pass to a mortal, but... well. Obviously we were wrong."

She couldn't understand a word her mother was saying. So much of it was wrong compared to the story she knew.

Her father wasn't a changeling child. He was the son of a

farmer from a different town who had met her mother in the market. The story had always made her heart warm in her chest because what were the odds of meeting your soulmate in a busy area of town?

"What?" she asked again. Her voice thin and reedy. "Father can't be a changeling. They're not mortal."

Eldridge responded first. "He was the mortal babe the fae stole to replace their child. So to us, yes. He's a changeling." He frowned and started pacing behind her mother. "I don't know what happens to those mortals. The magic here is strong and affects adults, but a child growing up here? He might as well have been fae."

No. None of this made sense. It wasn't right with what she had thought had happened and... And...

She couldn't breathe.

Finally, Freya shook her head and asked, "Why were you here, though? In the faerie realms at all?"

"Your father turned that night. He changed into the beast you saw when you found me, I suspect." Her mother leaned away from her, looking to Arrow, who gave her a little nod of encouragement. "He went through the portal in our woods. I followed him because I didn't want him to be here alone. I didn't know where he was going or why he would even try to find the faerie realms."

"And that's when you met the Spring Maiden," she whispered.

"She didn't want me to find him. As you know, time is... different, while traveling here. For your father, it was months before I got out of the portal and to the Spring Court. He'd already lost his mind and started killing." Astrid shook her head. "It was only a few pixies, but it was enough to set off the bloodlust. I went after him to see if he would listen to me, but the Maiden didn't want me to."

Freya could believe this part of the story. And though it wasn't the one she'd made up in her head, she also recognized that this was very much the truth. Her mother had come here intending to save her father. She'd failed, and thus, Freya had stepped into her shoes.

Frowning, Freya held her head in her hands. "Why did you think you could get him back? This is the faerie realm. It's nothing like our home, and finding him in an unknown land would have been impossible."

Her mother stared at her with wide eyes, as though she didn't recognize her own daughter. "Because I love him. I would have done anything to keep him alive, and I still will. I have no doubt that I will find your father and I will bring him home."

Freya recognized the fierce love in her mother. The kind of love that ended worlds and toppled kings from thrones.

Maybe that's where Freya had gotten it from.

Letting go of all the tension in her shoulders, she released her anger. At least for a little while. "All right, then. We'll find him together. But first, I think you need to see Esther."

"I wouldn't expect it any other way. Arrow told me that your father ran after you took me from my coffin." Her mother stood and her features hardened. She returned to the imposing, terrifying woman Freya knew her as. "Let's go to this Goblin King's court and find my husband together."

CHAPTER 28

As fierce as her mother was, a sleeping spell was much stronger. And so Astrid slept a lot on their trip back to the Goblin Kingdom.

Eldridge thought it was smarter to not travel through a portal. Too much magic in a mortal body was bound to hurt, he reasoned. Considering how long her mother had been affected by this spell, Freya wasn't going to argue.

They traveled in a small carriage all the way back to Eldridge's domain. And yes, it was as awkward as Freya feared it would be.

She hadn't expected talking to her mother to feel so... uncomfortable. They had a lot of mending to do in their relationship. Freya needed to work on her abandonment issues, and her mother needed to remember what it was like to be alive and not asleep.

Astrid kept her head against the carriage window and drifted in and out of the waking realm. Freya worried the spell wasn't entirely broken, but Eldridge insisted this was normal. Spells like that took a long time to wear off. And though most people would have thought the poor victim would be wide awake, often they wanted to return to sleep.

Apparently, a sleeping spell wasn't all that restful.

Freya watched the Goblin Castle appear on the horizon. The strange galaxy of stars appeared behind it, even though the sun was still out. The dark silhouette of the imposing building made the tension in her chest ease.

She was home. Even though her mother was a stranger and they had yet another person to save. At the very least, she was home.

The wheels rattled on the cobblestone and woke Astrid. Sitting up straighter, her mother rubbed her eyes and yawned. "Are we here?"

"We are." Freya watched the front gates open and saw two figures waiting for them in front of the door. One with a rat tail that waved behind him, and one with a fluffy white tail that wagged in excitement.

What would her mother think now that her baby girl wasn't human anymore? Freya would protect Esther from any words that would insult her looks. Esther was just as beautiful as she was before. No one would ever tell her otherwise.

The carriage stopped and Lux opened the door.

Her mother flinched away from the rat-faced boy who held out his hand as though nothing had happened. "Madame. Welcome to the Goblin Court."

To her mother's credit, she took Lux's hand. "Thank you. It's not at all like I expected."

"I imagine not." He helped her to the ground and then bowed low over her fingers. "Know that we are not a threat to you or your daughters. The two of them have made quite an impression in a very short amount of time."

Freya pressed her palm against her mouth to hide her smile. If Lux was trying to get on her mother's good side so she wouldn't mind her daughter being in love with a goblin, then he was doing a good job of it. He looked every inch a nobleman who was about to ask to court her daughter.

Good. Let him sway her mother first. He was much more terrifying to look at than Eldridge.

"Mother?" The shout echoed through the courtyard. Esther shot across the cobblestone and slammed into their mother with all the force of an avalanche, locking her arms around Astrid's waist and sobbing into her neck.

Maybe that's how it should have gone between Freya and Astrid. But she just couldn't do that.

Freya wished their reunion had been one full of tears and love. She would have loved to fall into her mother's arms and purge all the emotions the past few years had brought her. That had never been their relationship, though, had it?

Her mother had poured all her teachings into Freya's head. Not a single day went by when she wasn't trying to train Freya in some kind of lesson that made little sense but was important. Esther was the one who got the love. The hugs. The adoration and the bedtime stories.

Freya was supposed to take care of her sister. And Esther was the one to be taken care of.

Sighing, she turned to look at Eldridge and tried to muster a watery smile. "She's home now. Esther will be so happy to have her back."

He tucked a strand of hair behind her ear, brows furrowed and worry twisting his expression. "And you?"

"If I had known she was alive, I would have been searching for her just as I did Esther." Although, that would have proven much more difficult considering she had only been a child when her mother had disappeared. Traveling to the faerie realm might have been more dangerous when she was that young.

"Freya!" Esther shouted. "You did it!"

She waved a hand over her head awkwardly. "I did!"

Esther bounded to her side and grabbed her hands. "Now that we have Mother back, everything can return to normal. We'll be like a family again."

Why was she the one who always had to break her sister's

heart? Astrid was here. She could tell Esther all about the horrible things that had happened to their father, and that their lives weren't going to slow down any time soon.

No, she wouldn't be this person anymore. She didn't want to see the light die from Esther's eyes. Not when her sister was looking at her like a hero, yet again. As though Freya could defeat any monster that was thrown at her.

She liked it when Esther looked at her like that. It reminded her of all the times she had chased away nightmares.

Softly smiling, she ran her fingers through Esther's hair, settling all her flyaways back into place. "Mother has a lot to talk to you about, but I'll let you two get settled before we tell you anymore. Get her rested and well, while we clean up. Will you?"

"Of course." Esther's grin didn't waver. "It's so good to have her back. I never stopped believing she was alive, you know. I'm glad I was right."

Her sister ran off to grab her mother by the arm. Esther would drag the poor woman all over the castle before she finally let her sleep again. But this was what her mother had missed for all these years. Hopefully she would indulge her youngest daughter in listening to what Esther had to say.

After all, Esther had earned this time for the heartache and loss she had suffered.

Eldridge pressed his hand to the small of her back and nudged her toward the side of the castle. "Come with me. We'll let your sister handle your mother for the time being."

"Oh?" Her stomach flip-flopped. What did he want to talk with her about? Was this going to be a conversation about indulging in each other in that mining town?

Freya hadn't even had the chance to think about that. She had a bit, but really, now was the time for her to sit down and measure the repercussions. She'd slept with the Goblin King. Not many people did that. Or at least, not many mortals.

Now that she thought about it, though, maybe a lot of

people did. Maybe it meant nothing to him and she was over here worried that he was going to... to...

"Freya," Eldridge said with a chuckle. "I can see your mind racing. Would you follow me and see what I have to show you? Stop overthinking everything and just be for a few minutes."

Just be.

She could do that.

Freya trailed along behind him through a set of wrought-iron gates covered in ivy. She wondered how similar the layout of this castle was compared to all the others. Were the leaders together when they built their homes? Or did each castle have its own labyrinth-like quality that differed vastly from the others?

He led her into a small garden. This wasn't at all like the Spring Maiden's flowers. Instead of bright pinks and pastels like Freya was used to, this garden was filled to the brim with deep emerald colors and black petals. A garden of midnight blooms.

"How beautiful," she said.

And it was. She could feel the tension leaking out of her by the minute. No longer were her eyes overwhelmed by the sight of so much color and brightness. Instead, he'd given her the opportunity to ease into the shadows and be forgotten by the world. At least for a little while.

Eldridge drew her to a bench carved out of dark stone and set her gently on the surface. He knelt before her, staring up into her eyes, and holding her hands in his. "I know you're overwhelmed. So much has happened in such little time. I would be surprised if you knew how to handle this all without bursting at the seams."

Don't cry, she told herself. Don't cry because he's being nice to you.

She feared if she spoke, then all the tears would pour out of her. So Freya nodded sharply and stared down at their hands.

"I need you to know that I am here," he murmured. "Not as the Goblin King. Not as your rival or your companion in a quest to find your mother. I am here as the man who loves you."

His hands clenched on her fingers, forcing her to stay still when she might have ripped her hands out of his and retreated.

"No," Eldridge chuckled. "You aren't getting away so easily. I need to tell you this, Freya. And you need to hear it."

"What if I'm afraid?" she whispered.

"Of what?" Eldridge leaned back with wide eyes. He stared at her as though she'd admitted to having lost her mind.

"Of being a disappointment to you. I'm not a faerie, or... Maybe I am. I don't know." Freya slid her fingers from his grip and tangled them in her skirts. "I won't be like anyone else you've ever been involved with. And everything I do will probably confuse or frustrate. I'm afraid you'll wake up in a few months, or perhaps years, and that you'll want someone else."

"Ah." He stood and sat down on the bench with her. Eldridge braced his elbows on his knees, stared off into the distance and nodded. "Yes, I suppose loving a mortal comes with its own complications."

At least he understood her thoughts. He would be disappointed eventually, in something that she did, or worse... who she was.

Freya swallowed hard and tried not to be too upset that he'd agreed so easily. But she had to expect that. After all, she was the one who had brought it up.

She opened her mouth to say she was going back to her room, only for him to interrupt her.

"Except..." He turned toward her, and the grin on his face didn't match what she had thought was running through his head. "It is rare for anyone to ever truly understand love. I know that when I look at you, I can feel my heart take flight. Every time you speak, my stomach lurches like I'm going to be sick, but it's an illness I desire. You touch me and I want to be a better man. Not just for you, but so I know that I deserve you in my life."

Tears built in her eyes again. How was she ever supposed to know how to deal with this man? He was trying so hard and she was struggling to even admit her feelings to herself. No matter how much she wanted to.

He cupped her cheek in his hand and grinned. "You don't have to say it back, you know. I don't expect that. But I want you to know and acknowledge that I would tear the stars from the sky for you. Every inch of your body is beloved by me. And I will rip apart anyone who dares try to take you from me."

Her lips parted in a sigh and he took advantage. Eldridge gently kissed her with all the passion he had kept in his heart.

She wanted to say it back to him. Every fiber of her soul screamed that she loved him too. Dearly. More than her own soul. But something stopped her. The words caught on her tongue and refused to come out no matter how hard she tried.

Eldridge slid his lips from hers, then pressed a kiss against her ear. "It's all right," he whispered. "I'll say it for you."

He kissed the highest point of her cheekbone. "I love you."

His lips glided down the sharp edge of her jaw. "I love you."

He pressed twin touches to her eyes. "I love you. I love you."

Freya kept her eyes closed and basked in the knowledge that not only was she loved, but she was safe here in his arms. And she might not be safe forever, but in this moment she was.

Tomorrow they would start figuring out how to save her father. Tomorrow she would walk into a room where her mother was alive with unfinished business between them.

Tonight, she would indulge herself in the delicious, forbidden touch of the Goblin King.

ABOUT THE AUTHOR

Emma Hamm is a small town girl on a blueberry field in Maine. She writes stories that remind her of home, of fairytales, and of myths and legends that make her mind wander.

She can be found by the fireplace with a cup of tea and her two Maine Coon cats dipping their paws into the water without her knowing.

Subscribe to my Newsletter for updates on new stories!
www.emmahamm.com

facebook.com/EmmaHammAuthor

twitter.com/EmmaHammAuthor

instagram.com/emmahammauthor

THE STORY CONTINUES...

Of Werewolves and Curses!

Click Here to start Reading!